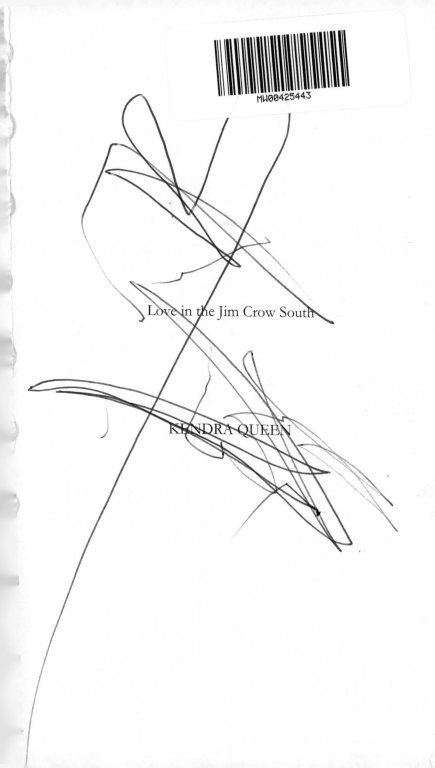

Love in the Jim Crow South

KENDRA QUEEN

DEDICATION

For P, my dreamer.

CONTENTS

ACKNOWLEDGMENTS

Thank you to my readers. I appreciate your support
more than I can say!

PROLOGUE

The letter came on a Sunday. It was not an ordinary Sunday, though in all outward appearance it behaved like one. It was hot, for starters, and the Freedom Church was bellowing and hollering like the rapture was upon them. The impious ones sat on the stoops and observed the Sabbath of rest. They listened to their brothers and sisters in the church and kissed their teeth.

As the day wore on the church-people screamed in louder ecstasy. And it made the people who were not in Church, those whose duty it was to sit and observe, curl their lips back and say unpleasant things. They felt hot and disturbed. Something nasty was on the wind. Something like a curse.

The mailman passed these watchers of Rue Cher and squatters and made his way up a high hill. The sun was a fearsome thing in Louisiana, but the humidity was worse. Swamp country. He was pouring sweat by the time he cleared the hill and posted the letter to the black man standing at the gate to collect it.

The black man, dressed in a sharp brown uniform, brought the letter to a maid sweeping the porch outside. The maid was black as well, and so was the butler she delivered the letter to. In fact almost everyone in the house had some color, but this was nothing unusual in Louisiana. It was a pair of white hands that broke the seal on it at last, and there the letter's journey ended and our story began.

Renard Mauricette scanned the contents of the envelope with growing distaste. His sister Fiona sat in the corner, watching him fretfully over the top of her magazine. Like everyone in the Mauricette household she feared her brother's temper, which, ever since he had returned from the war, threatened to spill over into violence at the slightest provocation.

The letter read:

Dearest Renard,

You thought you had seen the last of me; I have come to tell you that you have not. Crawl back into your little swamp hole all you like. I will always know where to find you.

In one week I will be returning to my father's house. We must put this absurd quarrel behind us, darling. Father won't be pleased to hear how you've embarrassed me. Let's hope, for your sake, he feels forgiving this time.

These dramatics have gone on long enough. I'm starting to get bored, and soon I may get angry. I will see you soon.

Love,
Amelie.

Renard crumpled the letter in his fist and threw it in

the empty fireplace. His face made a snarl.

"Who was it?" tittered his sister, as if she didn't know. Only two people could really make Renard look so dangerous, and one of them was dead.

"Amelie," he said. At the name his mother glanced up from her book.

"I don't suppose you're ready to take her back?" she said sharply. "It would mean you doing the smart thing, for once."

"I refuse," said Renard. "But she claims she's returning to Rue Cher. Come to throw the baby in my face, no doubt."

"You're a fool," declared his mother, which was her common refrain. "The girl is heir to the greatest fortune in Louisiana. A child with her-"

"She's a damned witch," interrupted Renard. "And the child isn't mine."

"You will not divorce her," said Madame Mauricette, her voice rising. The idea of divorce sent shivers down her spine.

"Be quiet, Mama."

"I will not let this house become a den of sin. Not on my grave. Not on your father's. Or by the Blessed Virgin-"

Renard left the room, his mother's shrieks ringing through the closed door. So Amelie was coming back, was she? The damned bitch. No wonder his leg was much worse today. He limped downstairs. The servants only watched him struggle; Master Renard refused all help from his affliction.

He entered the parlor and collapsed heavily in a velvet chair. The expression twisting his face might have been physical pain or mental aggravation. Likely both. The servants hurried on with their polishing and left. He supposed they were frightened of him, like most

5

people in this house. Like most people he met.

Renard cut a tall and imposing figure. Before the war he had even been handsome. Blue-black hair curled to his shoulders. He had the thin, lupine features of old French stock. Two hooded hazel eyes, thick-lashed, were thin and slanted almost like a cat's. They gave him a calculating expression; indeed, Renard was a calculating man.

Perhaps it was better to be calculating than handsome. His appearance had been ruined by a heavy dose of shrapnel to the chest, cheeks, and left thigh, courtesy of the war he had fought in. Now he walked with a loud, obvious limp. Deep furrows dug lightly into half his face, and heavily into half his chest. He was spoiled goods.

In reminder his injured leg gave a sharp pang. Like an eagle's talons digging into the flesh and striking bone. He grunted and clenched the handles of the chair.

Amelie was returning to Rue Cher, alright. He could

feel it.

Smoke and rich men have always loved high places. And Anjou Mauricette, Renard's great- grandfather, had been no different. The Mauricette mansion was built in 1790. Presently it sat atop a large hill. From its seat the house obtained a total view of the village of Rue Cher.

Rue Cher, indeed, was breathtakingly beautiful. But looks were deceiving. Looking out on the quaint village nested in the valley below, one might make the incorrect assumption that all its inhabitants lived in perfect harmony. In truth they did not. Blacks and whites lived on opposite sides of the river, literally and metaphorically. Over it all presided Renard's family. And though this network of lives and experiences intersected at many points, the three groups: wealthy whites, poor whites, and poor blacks, despised each other in turn.

The Mauricette house itself was a monstrous testament to both hubris and unoriginality, for it had been designed in the same style of many French Creole plantations in the region. Inside it, a nauseating labyrinth of rooms, compartments, closets and hallways confused all but the people who lived there.

Today its oppressive atmosphere threatened to choke Renard. He pulled on riding boots and lurched towards the stables. These days he didn't do much riding, but it was the one place on the property no one could threaten to bother him. His mother and sister detested riding and refused to trust the new automobiles.

"Hello, Mister Renard," said Ma Julie the cook, emerging from the outdoor kitchen. She was carrying a heavy pot of stew with two cloths wrapped around the handle.

"Hello Julie," said Renard. "Be careful going inside.

They're on the warpath."

Julie nodded and bumped along.

His leg was a rod of fire shooting out of his hip joint. Renard had been to many, many doctors. He'd had many, many doctors come to him. They all gave him the same verdict. They did the same things. Poked, prodded, pronounced. Nothing we can do. So sorry.

He couldn't care less about his appearance. Besides, many men had gotten it worse. He'd known one corporal who had his whole lower jaw blown to smithereens by a shelling.

It was just hard to accept his disability. Before the war Renard had been an active man. Now he couldn't take ten steps without feeling like some iron-clawed giant was twisting his leg off. He knew well if he didn't master the pain with grueling and regular exercise, he might well spend the rest of his life bound to the house. Becoming old and fat and petulant, like his father. The thought made him so depressed he couldn't stand it.

Halfway to the stable he collapsed in frustration under a spreading Magnolia tree. Sweat soaked the collar of his shirt.

One doctor, the most useful of the lot, had instructed him to breathe through such pains. He did so now and allowed his mind to wander.

In France his entire view of the world had changed. Not just the brush with death and getting crippled. He had rubbed elbows with men of the lower class, working men and boys. Black men from England, educated black men from France, and even a Colored Regiment from Georgia. In those nights there hadn't been much to do but talk. An ever-curious Renard had fluttered from group to group, when the time was spare, and made talk with folks from all backgrounds.

He'd come back a different man. Renard had once loved this house as a child, with its palacial rooms, sweeping staircases and ever-rotating cast of servants.

But now he saw it for what it was: a sprawling monument to man's arrogance. These Louisiana sugar barons and cotton kings didn't know the first thing about life or suffering. And it was not wood that held up this mansion, but bones.

"Damned cynic," he muttered to himself. One of the servants approached him with a pitcher of water. He recognized the man as John.

"Thirsty?" asked John.

"Like the devil," said Renard. "Come, sit with me."

John and Gaspard would have been the same age. The stocky black man had worked at the Mauricette house for a long time.

"You're hurtin'," observed John. He sat.

"It's nothing," said Renard. He drank deeply from the pitcher.

"What the doctor say?"

"Nothing he could do," said Renard. "Just got to bear it. But I knew that."

They sat in silence, listening to the cicadas. John eyed the stony-faced young man next to him. He remembered well the happy boy Renard had been, before old Gaspard shipped him off to fight in Europe's war. John didn't care much for white folks in general, but he had what you might call a camaraderie with the young master. Renard was not churlish or violent- only distant.

"You ever thought," said John carefully, "'bout seein' someone from the village?"

"You mean one of your doctors?"

"Just an idea," said John, already regretting the suggestion. "Sometimes you know, the natural stuff works better. The old folks do say that."

Renard imagined the scandal it would cause if word got out he had seen a negro witch-doctor. He opened his mouth to refuse, but the sharp pain stabbed up his leg once more, and he found himself agreeing. What did it matter if he saw a Negro doctor? He didn't care what these people thought of him.

"Can I see him tonight?"

"Oh yeah," said John, smiling. "I'll take you to her."

"Her?"

The screech of Madame Mauricette interrupted. "John! John! Where the devil are you?"

"Lord have mercy," muttered John. The old butler got to his feet with a heavy sigh, and ambled back across the yard.

Renard stood up too, and began to hobble toward the stables.

13

He was surprised to see someone there waiting for him.

It was a balding man with deep green eyes and a lecherous gap tooth. Dressed in exaggerated finery. Louis Mordant and Renard's father had been close friends. Renard, for his part, couldn't stand the gentleman.

Renard was not a superstitious man. But his dislike for the Mordants had existed long before they became intertwined in his life, as merely a gut feeling that was eventually confirmed by steady observation. It was rumored that the Mordant family dealt heavily in witchcraft. A strange group of people indeed. Extremely reclusive. Extremely wealthy. If someone slighted them their revenge seemed to take curious forms, like a sudden illness of the offender, a sudden streak of bad luck. Or a lamed leg.

"Ah, Renard," said Louis Mordant, stroking the nose of a strawberry roan. He did not turn to greet the young master.

"Mordant," said Renard. "I was not aware you were here. No one announced you."

"Your mother gave permission. I came to get something of your father's."

"Father's things are in storage."

"No, no. This was something very special. He meant for Amelie to have it. It is why she has returned."

"Indeed?" said Renard. His father had been one of the biggest proponents of he and Amelie's marriage. Wedded to the daughter of his best friend. A match made in heaven, eh?

"Tell me what it is and I will fetch it for you," said Renard. "But after this neither you nor Amelie will not set foot in this house."

The other man's eyes sparkled. He looked, as always, like he wanted nothing better than to cut Renard's throat. But his tone was icily polite. "It is- a book. A journal. My daughter wanted it for her studies. But I do not know where it is. I came to search-"

"I have seen no such journals."

"Surely you have overlooked-"

"I doubt it," said Renard swiftly. "But if I find a journal I will deliver it to you. I personally never knew father to look at any book that didn't have dirty drawings plastered over the pages. But I am sure you know better than I what Amelie wants. Or the workings of my father's mind."

"Certainly," said Louis. "I also meant to ask about something else. Some land you have down in Rue Cher."

"Land?"

"Yes. But I'll send my men to discuss it. It seems you aren't in the mood for talking."

Mordant pushed past the younger man and left the stables. He was angry. Renard did not care.

He got the strawberry roan out and led it to the center of the pastures. He let the horse go and lay down in the grass. He felt imprinted on the earth, connected to everything. But also very alone.

"I'm going to get this damn leg fixed," he said aloud. "And then I will leave Rue Cher for good."

Several things fluttered through his mind. He missed Boston. He hoped this 'doctor' of John's knew what she was doing. When it came down to it, Renard would try anything.

CHAPTER ONE

They brought the man in while Eva was tending the garden. She smelled the blood before she saw them, fresh and hot, the smell of metal. When she looked up two men were on the path, walking abreast, holding Trout Jenkins between them. Trout's right foot was sliced up pretty bad and leaking blood all over the grass.

"Lord ha' mercy," Eva declared, rising to her feet. "What happened?"

"He was playin' the fool, that's what," declared Chillo Jenkins, brother of the injured. "Thought he could mess around with that stupid old plow. Nearly sliced his toes off."

Eva had the men bring Trout inside and lay him on her porch. She cleaned her hands and came over.

"How long you been bleedin'?" she asked Trout.

"Ten minutes," he said weakly.

She took a look at the wound, twisting his ankle this way and that. Trout hissed and bit his lip. Eva went inside the house. She didn't need to think too hard about it. The wound looked worse than it was. With a wooden spoon she scooped up some ash from the fireplace into a cup. Then she went under the house and spooled up a nest of cobwebs.

"Work this together," she said, thrusting the two at Chillo. She went back inside and got some powdered yarrow. You could use Yarrow for a lot of things. Toothache, bites, burns. And puncture wounds. Though Eva could have done without the smell.

"You got any shine, Evie?" asked Trout nervously. Eva always made him nervous. And no wonder- the look she fixed him with was downright intimidating.

"Naw. You can't be bleedin' all over my porch and gettin' drunk off my hooch to boot."

"Ma used to say you put nine rusty nails in a pot of hooch and let it sit under three full moons. You can use it to cure almost anythin'. From fevers to headache and digestion," said Mitch Davis. He watched Eva work in fascination.

Whenever folks came to see Eva, they did one of two things. They either sat silently until she finished or tried to talk about one of their own family remedies and get her opinion. They learned to read her reactions. A raising of the eyebrows meant she thought it was good. A pursing of the lips meant the opposite. And a long, flat stare meant she wanted you to hush up and let her work in peace. She usually delivered the latter.

She had heard of that remedy with the nails and the hooch before. She didn't want to knock Old Ma Davis, so she said nothing, though she thought it a load of hogwash. Nothing some old rusty nails in some dirty old shine would do but give you an ulcer.

In two twos she had the yarrow powder sprinkled over the cobweb thatch and packed into the wound. For a bandage she used a strip of old muslin. Then she pulled a clump of herbs from her pocket. "Drink this in a tea every morning 'till it gets better. If you run out, send Chillo back for more."

"Thank you, Evie," said Trout weakly. She patted him on the leg. It had taken her all of five minutes.

"No trouble. Can you boys walk him home?" she asked.

"I can," said Chillo. "C'mon. Giddup." He slid an arm under his brother's armpits and hoisted him to his feet and off the porch.

"Thank you, Evie," said Trout again, smiling through his pain. "You 'bout as sweet as peaches and sugar. I could just kiss you."

"Go on home, you fool," said Eva.

They went back down the path. This was the second time this month she'd had to treat Trout Jenkins for his clumsiness. If she didn't know any better she'd say he busted himself up on purpose.

But she looked out at the receding figures fondly. Eva felt responsible for everyone in Rue Cher, in some way. She hoped his wound would heal soon so he could get back to his farm.

Mitch Davis stayed behind. Eva looked at him but said nothing. The subject of payment was never overtly discussed, and it was not Eva LaLaurie's way to ask or demand. She treated and healed, and the good people of Rue Cher did whatever they could in return. Trout was Mitch's friend. It seemed he would be covering the debt today.

"That garden need some weedin'," he offered.

"It sure does."

"Let me finish it for you."

Eva's smile nearly melted his heart into his drawers. "Thank you, Mitch."

She turned on her heel and went inside, humming. The smell of lavender or rosemary always seemed to trail about her skirts. Mitch resigned himself to the garden. Planter's work was over for the day anyway. And he'd rather spend the rest of the day under Miss Evie's window.

Eva LaLaurie was a handsome woman, in the soft, countryish way that women from Rue Cher were handsome. She had a thick waist, thick thighs and a smooth, open face. Her hands were strong and capable. She had brown skin the color of a roasted chestnut, or a dark kind of amber. Skin like the earth. Wide, deep black eyes could either cut you to the quick or melt you down to butter. Those eyes haunted the thoughts of many in Rue Cher.

Weeding the garden didn't take Mitch long, and Eva had a glass of lemonade ready for him when he was done. He took it back to the little porch and she sat next to him. Eva liked Mitch; he was quiet and kind. Mitch would have taken a bullet for Eva.

The dusk rose up around them with the sweet heat of a long summer. The air hung heavy. Crickets made chorus in the swamp, and cities of fireflies came out to flaunt those caches of starlight at their waists, twirling and spinning in secret dances.

"Ain't you thought of marryin', Eva?" Mitch Davis asked her. He kept his voice light and teasing.

She shrugged. "If I got married, I'd lose my medicine. The way I see it, I'm already married to this place. Y'all like my own children."

As they talked her cousins Sam and Esau came ambling up the path. They held two buckets between them and were barefoot and mud-splattered from heel to waist. Catfishing, most likely. Sam was twelve, Esau thirty, but they were almost of a height. When they saw Mitch and Eva they raised their arms in greeting.

"Ho!"

"Y'all come from the swamp?" asked Eva.

They came up to the gate. "Yeah. Want a fish?" offered Sam.

Laughing, the woman jumped off the porch and reached out for the fish he dangled on a piece of old twine. About the size of her forearm it was, and slippery as an eel. As Eva ducked inside to put it on some salt, Esau leaned on the fence post and called out a conversation.

"Y'all hear 'bout what happened at the river?"

"Nooo, you gonna tell us?" said Eva, returning. She took a seat next to Mitch and wiggled her toes.

"Only if it's funny," said Mitch. "I done seen enough serious shit for today. Trout nearly cut his leg off."

"Oh, it's funny."

"G'on then."

Esau took his weight off the fencepost and bent down to pluck a tall weed. He stuck it in his mouth. "Michael and Buck and Tom were just down by the beach this afternoon. When here come this white man dressed all up like the fourth of July."

"You was there?" asked Mitch.

"Naw, heard it from Dewey. Anyway here comes this white man, and he say, 'What is you coons doin' on my property?' So Tom says, excuse me mister gentleman sir, what you mean this is your 'property'?"

"His property!" Mitch exclaimed indignantly. It was a point of pride that all of East Rue Cher was owned by negroes.

"That's what Tom said. He says excuse me sir, what you mean this is yo' 'property'? This side of the river is owned by black folks. That's your side over there."

"Oh Lord," said Eva wearily.

"And then the man says 'what's that, Jim?' So Tom raise his voice and repeat the question."

They shook their heads. Tom Shanter's tongue had its own reputation.

"What did whitey do?" asked Mitch.

"Ol' white man just picks up his cane and cracks Tom a good one 'cross the spine. And all the men, you know, just start bawlin'. But the white man just pull himself up tall like this-" Esau drew himself up- "and says, 'it ain't my land yet, but soon or later you dirty niggers gon' have to get off it and make some space."

"Whew," said Mitch.

"Lord," said Eva again.

"Tell them what Tom did," Sam piped up.

"I'm tellin' it, Sammy. Anyway, Tom tol' this white man he knew a lady that could put some hands on him. She could make his ol' pink pecker turn black an' fall right off."

"Oh no," moaned Eva.

"An' that cracker turned as pale as the moon. You know how they get 'bout that witch stuff. So away he goes off in a hurry, an' he's got his hand on his head like this-"

Esau burst into laughter at his own imitation, and the

rest of them broke up too. "And he's so puffed up he trips on Buck's fishin' pole and lands clean on his behind."

"And then what he do?"

"He hollered like he was raisin' the dead and said he'd fetch Tom an' his boys something good. So Tom says he'd like to see that ol' white man try it. That old bastard was so heated he took another step, got himself sucked down a mud hole and lost his walkin' stick. Just yellin' blue Jesus the whole time. So finally the boys felt bad for 'im and went over to help. But he thought they was about to kill 'im, and he kept cussin' and yellin' so bad they just left him there. Buck said when he did get out he was so scared he'd done went and pissed himself."

Esau couldn't finish, and they all dissolved into cackling. Sam filled in the rest of the story. The men had snatched up their poles and hotfooted it back to Rue Cher, bellowing with laughter and telling Tom Shanter he would live and die a fool.

"Just watch," said Mitch, wiping away tears, "soon or later the white folks gon' come for this place. Just like they did in DuPont."

"They'd never," Eva snorted. "This place ain't nothin' but swamp."

"Don't put it past 'em," said Esau. "Don't put anythin' past 'em."

And that was the law by which they all lived, wasn't it? You could just never tell what these white folks would do next. They were unpredictable as wild dogs, and four times as cunning.

They jawed for a while. Soon Mitch got off Eva's porch and went down the way with Esau. Only little Sam stayed behind.

He was a tall, frail-looking boy with large round eyes like Eva's. One of those eyes had been clouded from an early childhood sickness. Little Sam had been born 'in the caul', as they said. He could see things most people couldn't. Eva had hopes that he would take to her healing practice. Every doctor needed an apprentice, and she was grooming Sam to be hers.

"You gonna fry that fish?" he asked, standing on one foot to scratch a mosquito bite with the other.

"You know I am," she said. Eva's love of fried fish was well-known through the village. "You hungry?"

"Yes Ma'am." Sam put down his bucket and came through the gate.

"Ah-ah," said Eva. "Not with them dirty feet. Wash 'em."

She bustled inside and started on the fish. An old skillet on the fire, and some oil...and two fat potatoes, with good sprinkles of seasoning and hot red peppers. An expensive meal, to be sure. The oil Eva got from her friend Mamie, for giving her something for the pain in her bad breast. The skillet she got from Joe

Black for setting his broken thumb. Everything in Eva's cabin, as a matter of fact, she got from helping somebody. Even the dress she wore and the two shined shoes in the armoire which she only took out on special occasions.

Her best paying customers were the people of East Rue Cher, though Eva treated white folks sometimes too. These white folks came across the river to see her. They were stingier, but paid in real money.

Sam cleaned the fish for her and she seasoned it well with pepper and salt and cayenne. Then she slid it in some flour meal and had it popping grease in the pan before you could say yes please.

"I saw a fish as big as Esau today," declared Sam, his nose twitching at the warm smell of the fish. "Nearly bit my pole in half. Big ol' catfish."

"Aw, and you didn't get it for me?" she laughed. "I been meanin' to get some catfish whiskers."

"What you do with 'em?"

"Gotta be a nine-year old fish. Gotta be long whiskers. You bury 'em under the doorframe of a new house, you get nine years of luck. Or you give 'em to a man minced up in his soup. Makes him potent." She winked, and Sam giggled.

She served the fish and fried potatoes on mismatched china plates. They ate on the porch again. The dying sun washed all the flowers in deep purples and pinks. Eva thought about how Sam's appearance was becoming a regular thing at her place.

"How your family doin', Sammy?"

"They good," said Sam. He tossed a flake of fish at Boots the cat, who showed up for her evening scavenge.

"You sure?"

"Yeah," said Sam. He frowned, looking out down the

path. "Who you think that is?"

She squinted; despite her weekly compresses, her eyes were not the best, and getting worse.

"Why, it look like Butler John." Butler John, not to be confused with Barber John, who lived near the white side of town and pulled teeth and cut hair.

Sam put down his plate. "He got a white man with him."

"A what? They don't never come so late."

"Fancy white man," said Sam. "Look, he got a cane! They comin' to see you?" He thought of the white man from Esau's story.

"I never," said Eva. She took their empty plates inside and hurried to wash her hands and face. No good to greet a customer looking like she'd been sucking up fish grease. Sam, following her example, wiped his mouth quickly with his sleeve.

"Ho!" John greeted. Still in his butler's uniform, he would have cut a fine figure among the loose overalls and shoeless feet that other men of Rue Cher wore every day.

Eva raised her arm in greeting despite her annoyance. She always had to mentally prepare herself to deal with white folks. And she didn't like bringing them in her house if it wasn't spotless. Why give them any reason to talk?

The men came closer and Sam gave a startled gasp.

"What's the matter?" hissed Eva.

"Don't let him in the house," Sam whispered urgently. "He's got somethin' on him."

"What you mean?"

"Somebody put work on him. A spell."

"Who? John?"

"Naw. The white man. I can see it plain as day."

Eva's hands twisted in her skirt as the men came through the shabby little gate. If Sam was right, which of course he was, someone had put a curse on the white man. She might bring the spell right into her house if she let him in without cleaning it off first. But she couldn't bar him from the house- he might take offense...

"Hello, Miss Eva," said Butler John. "This is Mister Renard. He was hopin' to be your customer today."

"How do you do," said Eva, inclining her head politely. "John didn't tell me he was gonna bring a...friend."

The "friend" tipped his hat, uncovering a shock of curly black hair. He was tall, very tall. And Eva recognized him. Her gut twisted in shock. This was one of the Mauricettes, she was sure. The white folks on the hill.

He wore a pressed linen shirt under a buttoned vest, some simple brown trousers and shined brown brogues. A signet gold ring flashed subtly on the same hand that gripped an ivory-handled cane. This was not a cane for flash and show; he leaned on it heavily. To the normal eye he appeared a regular citizen of Louisiana high society. To Eva's eye he appeared a man in pain. And to Sam...

"Can I help you?" asked Eva.

The white man's eyes darted to and fro, taking everything in. Her overgrown garden, the purring cat on the porch, the bare feet of her and Sam, and the lingering smell of fried catfish and potatoes. She set her jaw and affirmed herself: You run an honest practice. You got nothin' to be ashamed of.

John opened his mouth to speak, but the white man put in first. "You can. I'm here for my leg, and John said you could help me."

"Sure," she said. "Sure I can. Wait just a minute."

She ducked inside to set up the room. Young Sam moved a step ahead of her. He hauled out her Patient's chair and footrest, and put some cinnamon to boil in the low coals of the fire.

"You still gonna let him in?" he hissed.

Eva nodded. She had a policy of never turning anyone away. White man or no, cursed or no.

"I got no choice. We'll have to make do."

Butler John left them to it and went to see his sister down the way after helping the Mauricette inside; at her insistence he leaned on her to get up the two steps into the room. When he passed over the threshold she repressed a shudder. She hoped she could handle whatever she'd just invited into the house.

The white man's clothes were a size too big. Meaning he had lost weight but hadn't bothered to get them tailored. She appraised his face quickly. Something wrong in his mind too, then, some kind of sadness. He sank into the chair with a quick moan. The left leg stuck out stiffly in front of him. She saw the sweat that beaded on his forehead and the way he clenched the arm of the chair. He doffed his hat with his other hand.

"So you are the healer?" he said.

"Sam," said Eva, "Go on outside."

Sam left.

Eva sat on a little stool. "Yes sir, I am. My name is Eva LaLaurie. You can call me Eva."

"John told me you fixed things. What kind of things?"

As his eyes had surveyed the exterior of her little cabin, now they scanned its insides. They swept over her rows of bottles along the shelves, bottles she had scavenged from dumps, cleaned, and filled with her medicines. Next he eyed the rows of drying herbs around the wall. The bubbling pot of cinnamon on the fire- the rare spice had been a gift from her friend, Nelson. Her cornhusk pallet lay in the corner. Eva ate, slept and did her medicines in the same room. Though cramped, it was immaculate.

"I tend to almost everything," she said politely. "Tell me what's the matter with you."

He blinked at her frank way of talking. "Well," he said slowly, "It's my leg. Obviously."

"Right."

"Got busted up in the war by some shrapnel. That's the little bitty metal things-"

"Yes sir," she said crisply, "I know what shrapnel is."

An awkward silence. "Oh." He flushed. "Well- the doctors said it was an infection gone wrong. Somethin' to do with the nerves..." his eyes flicked up to her. Would she know what he was talking about? Eva's eyebrows lowered, but she said nothing.

"Anyway, it hurts somethin' fierce almost every day. I can't use it, I can't walk on it...'Bout the only thing I can do is stay inside and sit down. It hurts to even ride."

"That must be very hard for you. And you want me to fix it?"

"Well, no," he said impatiently. "No one can fix it. I'd just like somethin' for the pain. John said..." he trailed off again.

She folded her hands in her lap. For a white man to come all the way to Rue Cher, especially one as rich as this one, he must either be desperate or a fool. He could have bought any doctor in the state to come see him. And he was a Mauricette, to boot- she recalled her grandmother had been one of their slaves, back in that long-ago time. She should have never let him past the gate.

Still. Eva never turned anyone away. And this white man seemed polite enough. She had no cause to be rude to him- yet.

"I'll need to see it," she said carefully. "The wound, I mean. Before I can put hands on it."

"The leg? Alright."

To her surprise, he got to his feet and started unbuckling his belt right in front of her. She blushed and looked away. He kicked off his shoes and stripped the trousers quickly. Flushing deeply but determined, he resumed his seat.

Eva then and there decided to treat him like any of her Rue Cher patients. She cleared her throat and squatted next to him, tracing the skin with a gentle touch.

The scar was a hole. A cavern, like the imprint of a child's fist in clay. It impressed itself in the hard flesh of his left thigh. Now it was knotted and healed over, pulling the surrounding skin into its horrible vortex of damaged nerves and cells. There was another, smaller hole in the calf. Smaller scars spread out from the nucleus of this scar tissue. She suspected the entire left half of his torso, much like his face, would be speckled with these marks.

"You survived this?" she said.

"Indeed," he said, in a tone that said, *unfortunately.*

"Then you're a lucky man."

"Lucky enough that you can help?"

She straightened. "I'm no surgeon."

"I know. I won't take morphine or opium or anything they give me. I won't be bled. I've seen what it does. I just want you to find something else. Anything. One of your...remedies. For the pain." He was begging her, though trying to make it seem like he wasn't.

Eva laid a hand on his calf open-palmed. He flinched at her touch this time, but didn't pull away. His hooded eyes stared fathomlessly down into hers.

"I want to be honest with you, Mr. Renard."

"Please."

"I think this problem got two sides. There's the physical, and there's somethin' else."

"Don't tell me," he scorned, "It's all in my head."

She shook her head, annoyed at his tone. "Yes. I mean- no sir. Not really. That ain't what I'm sayin'. I'm sayin...Is there anyone who might want to do you ill?"

His eyebrows raised sharply. "What do you mean?"

Eva nearly balked at his tone, but she was too firm in her convictions to coat the truth as she saw it, not even for white folk. It was not her way. "I mean, do you got enemies? Someone who wants to hurt you?"

"Yes," he said quietly. "Why?"

"Somebody put a bad mark on you," she told him. "And it's stoppin' that leg from gettin' better. I aim to fix that, with your allowance, when I fix the leg."

He turned his palms skyward. She could tell he didn't believe her, but his curiosity at this point far overpowered his skepticism.

"I have nothing to lose. Do what you can."

Eva set to work immediately. She called Sam back inside, and the young boy sat in the corner to observe. His little face had twisted into a deep frown.

Eva moved like a clockwork doll. She had dealt with

much more serious cases before- but that didn't mean that what this man had was any less important to her. The hardest patients to deal with were the ones whose soul had gone wrong along with the physical body. She aimed to fix that.

The first problem she could see was the tension in the muscle in the upper thigh, where the deepest scar tissue had rooted. This muscle was kept taught at all times, sending pain through the entire leg. All the 'fibers' of the body, as Eva called them, were connected that way. To heal one part of the body sometimes you had to tweak another. She padded to her herb collection and scooped up the oft-used mason jar of grease. The metallic smell of camphor filled the air when she opened it. This was the carrier. A dollop on a china plate, and in went a dash of cayenne, bishop's wort, and something else. Eva never labeled anything and she didn't use measurements. Sam could only watch her closely.

She bore the interesting-smelling concoction back to her patient and seized a gooey handful. He eyed her with growing apprehension.

"Easy now," she told him, and slapped it on the wound.

He jolted in the chair, but she held him firmly and began to massage the torn muscle with steady pressure. He hissed through his teeth and sank back in the chair. Eva used her palms to grasp the meat of the thigh and the thumbs to work in the balm. Despite his injury, the muscles of the leg were still handsomely formed. He had a compact, strong body, lithe and supple as an athlete's.

She massaged in the medicine for several minutes until she saw his tensed shoulders lower and sink into relaxation.

"Can you hear me?" she said quietly.

"Yes," he murmured.

"Good. That's good. Just listen to the sound of my

voice."

The crickets chirruped outside. Sam breathed through his mouth. The old house creaked and settled. Camphor and cayenne and cinnamon, and another scent...the deep, ancient smell of the swamp, coming on a sudden breeze. Renard Mauricette twitched. "I'm listening."

"Good," said Eva. Her thumbs dug deeper into the muscle. He flinched, but stayed put. "I'm gonna count down from ten," said Eva, "And the lower I count, the more you're gonna sink right here into this chair. Take a breath on my every word. In, out. Don't say nothin', just listen."

Sam eyed her fearfully, but didn't dare interrupt. That was the first rule of working with his cousin. You never interrupted.

"Ten," said Eva, and she continued. "Nine. Eight."

With every word Renard Mauricette's head fell further

onto his shoulder. His breathing deepened, until it came slow and regular as a sleeper's. Perhaps he was asleep.

"Can you hear me?"

"Yes," he replied.

"Good. I want you to relax every part of your body. Start with your toes." She guided him up through his toes, calves, knees, groin, waist, all the way to the top of his head and tips of his fingers. When she finished he had melted into the chair. There was a disturbance outside; some men coming home from the fields. Renard moved not an inch.

Eva's hands left his thigh and moved to the hole in his calf. She spoke as if soothing a wild animal. Later on Renard would try to recall all of the words she had said to him, but they were blocked behind a wall of black mist, buried in the well of his subconscious. When he pulled away from the waking dream of her voice, she was sitting away from him on the stool, gazing intently at his face. She held a braided clump of grass in her hand; the end was smoking. He shuddered. It seemed he could still feel her hands touching his scar.

"How do you feel, sir?" she asked.

He blinked. Her face swam in his vision, and the face of the little boy in the corner. She looked friendly and calm, the boy did not.

"I feel...different."

A new smell permeated the cabin now, overpowering the cinnamon and the burning herb rope in her hand. A strong, grassy smell- and familiar.

"I would offer you tea," she said, "But I ain't have real fine wares here. Nothin' you would be used to. Best I just give you the herbs." She watched him. Of course this was a test, one of several she'd been giving him since he'd walked through the door. She was judging what kind of white man he was.

"I don't care," he said. He had drank out of worse before. "I would like some tea."

"Sure thing."

She moved to whatever was cooking in fat on the fire- the source of the herby smell. Now free from the pain, he observed her differently. As a woman.

She was young and attractive. In her early twenties. Unlike the scrawny women of Renard's High society, this woman was all slopes and curves. She had a high, full bosom. Her waist curved in waspishly before fluting out to an impressive derrière, which twitched when she walked even under the fabric of her modest house dress. She seemed soft and delicate, but Renard could tell she was not a woman to be trifled with.

"Can John fetch you back home in an hour?"

"I think so," he said. He eyed her from half-hooded

eyes. She was pretty in the face, too. Such open, smooth features. And her skin...

"Good. 'Cause after you drink this, you need to take a good long sleep." She strained the fat and slid it into the cup, then poured the boiled cinnamon water over it.

He already felt like he'd slept for ten years, but he accepted the tea anyway. Despite the heavy fat on the surface, and that she hadn't sweetened it, it went down his chest like sweet fire and he drained it in four gulps. Eva poured herself a mug and drank only the cinnamon, and Sam drank nothing. He just watched Renard Mauricette.

"One more thing," Eva said, once he finished. "I need you to sprinkle this water on your pillow every night before you sleep." She handed him a bottle the size of his little finger. "You Catholic?"

"Yes," he said, "why?"

"Then say a Hail Mary if you want." She chuckled. Then, jokes aside, she laid a hand on his arm. "How do you feel?"

His brow furrowed. He moved the bum leg stiffly. Then again. He got up and bracing on the wall for support, he bent his knee. It might have looked funny to some, the Louisiana gentleman standing in his striped undergarments and socks in the middle of a negro woman's kitchen, swinging his leg like he was taking a practice shot at kickball. But the expression that lit up his handsome face gave Eva LaLaurie's chest a funny squeeze. There was something heartbreaking, and not at all funny, about it.

"It hurts," he said, "But I can move it."

"Come back in three days," said Eva, "And I'll have some medicine ready. You kin rub it on there any time you feel queer. But don't let nobody else touch or see it. And don't get it in sunlight."

He nodded as if she were the most esteemed doctor

in all of Louisiana. "Anythin' else?"

"Yeah," she said, licking her lips and eyeing Sam, "Don't tell nobody you came to me. I keep a quiet business here. But if you feelin' poorly, come see me or tell Sam to fetch me right away."

"Thank you," said Renard. "You were not what I expected, to tell it true."

Eva's lips made a flat line. She nodded curtly and stepped outside with Sam while he dressed.

At last Butler John came to retrieve the strange white gentleman and escort him back where he belonged. Renard dug in his pockets and extracted a heavy leather sack. Sam's eyes flung wide as Renard counted out ten whole dollars in Eva's palm. Eva had never held that much money at once in all her born days. Even John made a quiet exclamation of surprise.

Renard was cool. He tipped his hat to her and put his arm on John's shoulder.

"Take me home," he drawled. "I think Miss Eva's potion is already wearin' me down."

Eva watched the two men head on up the path, her brow furrowed. What a strange man. What a handsome man. She had never expected a Mauricette to come through here.

"Is that Gaspard's son?" asked Sam.

"I believe so," said Eva.

"He ain't what I expected."

Only a while later, once the night had arrived in her black cloak, did they realize Renard Mauricette had forgot his cane.

CHAPTER TWO

Once, a long time ago, Renard Mauricette wanted to be a painter. He remembered going out with Geordie, his father's manservant, to the rolling hills and marshes of the Mauricette property that stretched for miles in every direction. Sometimes they might pick their way through the swamp to a private island where all kinds of wildlife gathered too. There he would set up his easel and paint the ibises and alligators and turtles, while Geordie amused himself by asking questions or strumming on Renard's old guitar (Had Madame Mauricette discovered Geordie plucking on her son's instrument, she would have sacked him on the spot). These times were the best in Renard's life.

He had never been an extroverted child, to play the rough games of the other white boys his age. He disliked their cruelty to animals, their cruelty to each other. And he found them boring. Beneath him. So Renard kept to himself and grew from a quiet boy to a quiet, haughty man.

When he was twenty he went to his father, Gaspard, and said, "I want to be a painter." He wished to attend the fine arts school in Paris, the kind his idol, Auguste Renoir, had nearly attended.

Gaspard nearly choked on his Oysters Benville. "Absolutely not."

"Why?"

"Because I damn well say so, boy," spat Gaspard.

At twenty-one, he asked again and received the same answer. But then Gaspard relinquished. If Renard would do a favor so small- marry the daughter of Laurence Mordant, only fifteen years his senior, but heir to a fortune of no inconsequential size that Gaspard had long had his eye on, then art school would be in his future. Naively, Renard accepted.

The rest, as they say, was history.

He'd gone to war. Escaping Amelie had been a worthy incentive. And he'd returned to his home in Boston not six months later with two holes in his leg, a scarred face, and another man sleeping in his bed.

Oh, but it had taken more than that to get him to leave. Still clinging to some feeble sense of honor, duty, or pride, perhaps, he had stayed with Amelie and the bastard she had fathered on him. And woken one night to find that his wife, his darling witch of a wife, tripling a morphine dose to inject directly into his cephalic vein.

He had leapt up with the intent to kill her. But of course, he had not been able to. Renard no longer had the taste for violence. Instead he left again. And since then his life had known no peace, and the pain no respite. Until two nights ago when he'd wandered through the door of a certain negro woman.

Eva woke the next morning to a sharp knock on her door. She jumped so bad Boots the cat, who had curled up at the foot of the bed, gave an ear-splitting yowl and sprang out the open window.

"Hang on just a minute," said Eva, stuffing her hair back under the wrap.

"Take your time, sugar, " the visitor drawled.

She opened the door. Of course, it would be Nelson.

Nelson was a Choctaw Indian. Old as the hills, and identified by the absurd blue cap he wore low over his brow. He and her mother had got along well. He knew the swamps and the woods like the back of his hand, and dug roots and herbs for Eva whenever he could. He had said on more than one occaision that she reminded him of his first wife.

"G'mornin Miss Eva," he said.

"Morning," she said, stifling a yawn. "Everythin' alright?"

"Well," said Nelson. He paused and frowned. "You got a cat in there?"

"Oh, that's Boots," said Eva. She hid the laugh from her voice- Nelson despised cats. "But I know you ain't come here 'bout her."

"Well," he said again. Nelson spoke as slow as molasses could crawl. "I came by this mornin' with the honey you ast me to bring a week ago. But then I realized I was comin' up too see you early, so I went to the swamps there and sat down and thought I'd catch myself a fish."

"Mmm," said Eva. He did smell rather fishy.

"After that I made my way back here quick as I could. And when I came back 'round to your place, there was this layin' right 'cross your doorstep."

He took something out from behind his back. Eva blanched and gasped.

Two crude poppets made of yarn, in black and white, sewn together hip to hip. They were soaked in what smelled like urine and bound in a woven rope of safflower.

"Don't touch it," she yelped to Nelson. "Get it away!"

"Now, now," he said, turning the thing over in his hands, "Don't worry. It won't harm me none. I'm just glad I got to it before you did. Let me take care of it."

She thanked him profusely. He shook his head. "All this to say that I forgot your honey back there in the swamp and I aim to go get it before the day's out. I'll leave it under your porch, mm?"

"It's no trouble," she said weakly.

He nodded as if he hadn't heard, and ambled away.

Someone wants to hurt me, she thought numbly. But who?

"So," said Sam, sucking the seed out of a juicy blue plum, "What you gonna do with that money?"

"The white man's money? I hope you didn't go flappin' yuh lips about it to your folks," said Eva mildly. "Or anybody 'round here."

"I didn't!" protested Sam. The juice ran down his face

and elbows. He spat the seed in her yard and wiped his hands on his trousers. "I was jus' wonderin'. Never seen that much money in my whole life."

"Me either," said Eva.

"You could get a dress," Sam suggested. In his childish mind he imagined Eva dressed up neat as you please like the fine creole ladies, with hat and shoes and parasol. Eva was as special to him as his own mother and sisters- even more special, because she didn't holler and beat him. He wanted her to have the finest everything. Sam dreamed of becoming a real doctor and having lots of money. He would put a proper porch on the house for Eva, yes sir, and fix that leaky tin roof too. They could have ice cream every day. Sam had never tasted ice cream.

Eva only snorted. "I'd rather get stuff for my doctorin'." She saw Sam's face fall, and nudged him. "I was gonna go down to Town today and get somethin'. You wanna come?"

His heart swelled to bursting. Wasn't that the best thing about his cousin? She never ordered or demanded- she asked. She treated him like a real man.

An hour later they set out. Eva in her best dress, starched and pressed and wearing her sole pair of shoes. Sam held her basket. The only ammendum to his attire was a busted pair of shoes. It was really the best he could do.

The apothecary was in West Rue Cher, where the white people lived. Black people knew better than to loiter here. If rich white folk hated negroes, then the poor whites hated them even more. And there were more poor white folks here than negroes.

"Why the white folks always gotta stare?" he muttered. They seemed like pale, milky insects to him. Their eyes followed them everywhere, like dull lamps of blue and green. Who could ever know what the white folks were thinking- but it couldn't be anything good.

"Pay 'em no mind," said Eva crisply. She held his shoulder firm, and her touch gave comfort.

"Ain't no law says we not allowed here." Yet.

While Nelson was visiting Eva, Renard was entertaining guests of his own. The two men sent by Louis Mordant to talk about land.

"It's very simple," said Broglie. He tapped the map laid out on the oak dest. Specifically, he tapped the crude drawing of Rue Cher.

"Get the negroes out. Get the white men in. They did it in Alabama. They did it in Mississippi. They've done it in parishes right here in the state. Can't see why you folks can't do it here."

And by you folks he meant Renard.

"You haven't a leg to stand on," said Renard. "Legally speaking. The people of Rue Cher own every acre of land down there."

"Unbelievable, Mr. Mauricette, that you have let it get to that state," said Broglie coldly.

"What state? They purchased it."

"And who sold it to them?"

"My grandfather," said Renard. "As was his legal right."

The looks on the two men's faces said it all. They thought him a disgrace. But a salvageable disgrace.

"With all due respect, sir," said Charles, Broglie's companion, "We shouldn't have to explain to you that in such cases as these, erm, the law is usually negligible. There are other ways to force niggers off land that don't involve tiresome litigation. Quicker ways."

"I see," said Renard. His dark eyebrows lowered. "As in force, you mean? Lynchings? Burnings? Rape?"

"Yes." Charles' eyes sparkled at the prospect. "We don't need to put it plainer, sir."

Renard had gotten the measure of the two of them from a single glance. Charles St. Joseph, a bulky man in a hideous tweed suit, and his companion Broglie, in spectacles and bowtie, the refined half of the two. Likely Broglie was the brains behind this endeavor, and Charles the muscle. And it all tied back to Louis Mordant.

He had seen and heard of men like this all across the Southern states, who menaced negroes off their property to acquire it for themselves, to then lease out to white tenants. Many of the black folk now fleeing the South to the Northern cities were escaping people like Charles and Broglie.

He doubted the people of Rue Cher would be so easily persuaded.

"But why are you coming to me for help?" he asked. "I have no control over what these people do."

They looked at him like he was a fool. "You are the richest man in the county," said Charles bluntly. "Of course we need your help."

Renard felt a sudden surge of irritation. He steepled his fingers and leaned across the desk. "Let me make it plain," he said, "there will be no evicting of negroes from Rue Cher. No intimidation, no threats. I've seen what the Klan is doing across the state. I won't have that here. Understand?"

"There was a lynching here just three months ago," Charles shot back.

Renard ignored him, and Broglie stepped in, to smooth things out in his oily voice. "I would inquire about your reasoning, Mr. Mauricette."

"Simple," said Renard tersely. He should not feel the need to justify himself to these men. "I am a pacifist. I fought one war in France. I won't have another on my doorstep."

There was a silence. He had reminded them that he was a veteran; he was deserving of their deference.

"Very well," said Broglie crisply.

But Charles was not so cool. "With all due respect—you'd have members of your own race fester in that town over the river while the negroes sit pretty on this fine piece of earth right under you. A shame, Mr. Mauricette. A damned shame."

"I would hardly call it festering. The whites have a hospital. Decent roads, a water system, sewage. Why, they're even getting electricity put in. You know what the people in Rue Cher have? Nothing."

"Never thought I'd see the day when a white man would put his neck out for some dumb negroes," Charles grumbled. "A damned shame, for certain."

Renard held on to his temper- barely. Broglie's slimy attitude and Charles and his due respects could be damned. "Then it is my shame to bear. I won't repeat myself." He moved to his feet and showed them the door. "Good day. And tell Louis Mordant I'll hear no more of his harebrained schemes. I am not my father."

He heard them hissing like snakes on the way out. He could imagine their talk. Who would have thought the son of old Gaspard, a friend to the negroes?

"Fetch the horses, boy!" Charles roared at Butler John impudently. Had Renard heard him there might have been hell to pay. But the young Mauricette had resigned himself to his study once more, and it would be a while before he emerged again.

As Eva and Sam walked down Mungo Street a cool wind picked up. The money burned a hole in Eva's pocket. She had considered using it to make some fine repairs around her house. There was always something that needed mending, hammering, nailing, adjusting.

But Eva had long had her eye on a very special item: a ready-made doctor's kit that hung on display at the Apothecary shop. The kit folded up into a neat Gladstone bag, with separate pouches for the different instruments, and a case for different medicines.

The Apothecary appeared somewhat of an oddity in a little town like this. The white people were poor, the black people were poorer. It was not the poor man's pennies that kept the doors open, either. The shop had in fact been founded by Louis Mordant, as a side hobby. He kept it stocked with the newest technologies. More than a few medical students from

71

the surrounding parishes had been known to frequent it.

They entered the shop. At the first flash of brown skin the shopkeeper's head bolted upright. Eva LaLaurie clenched her jaw. Even in her simple dress and cheap shoes, Eva maintained a sense of dignity. Sam had vouched to wait outside. One negro in a white man's shop would be quite enough trouble. No need to add another.

The shop itself stirred a sense of great wonder in Eva. Shelves ran along the walls from floor to ceiling, boasting bottles of every shape and color and size. Yellowed labels declared their names in regal print: Kickapoo Indian Oil. Hexamine. Triturate. Dr. Pierce's Favorite Prescription.

A cabinet behind the counter sported the most expensive of these, filled with chemicals Eva could not pronounce that all did different things. She saw syringes, pressurizers, stethoscopes, razorblades, a jar of murky water and leeches, a sealed glass dome with a miniature forest inside it...

Bird skeletons hung from the ceiling, perched on cabinets and drawer sets...And there in the display window- the Gladstone bag and the object of Eva's desire.

"Yes?" barked the shopkeeper, pulling her sharply to her senses.

"Erm. Yes. How much..." Her voice was faltered. She cleared her throat. "How much for that bag?"

"The what?"

"The doctor's bag. How much?"

He scanned her head to toe. The gears turned in his head. The negress was likely just here to buy something for her employer. Sent on an errand, yes, that was it. He stomped out from behind the counter.

"This?"

"Yes," she said.

"The bag alone is eleven dollars. The kit by itself is twenty-four dollars and thirty-nine cents."

Eva's heart sank to her shoes. If she left now, he would know she had come here to buy it herself. He would have a good laugh with his friends over the simple black woman who'd come in asking about a doctor's kit.

Still, Eva had the itch and she wasn't about to walk out empty-handed. No sir.

She jutted her chin up towards the bookshelf behind the counter. "And how much for them books?"

Realization dawned on his face; the shopkeeper's lips peeled back in a sneer. So she was just here for herself.

"You want to read them books?"

"Yes," she said.

"You can read?"

"I can read," confirmed Eva.

He stabbed a finger at the big one. Gray's Anatomy, 20th edition. "Twenty dollars."

"I'd like to see the cheapest one, please," she said.

But the man had had enough. "Time for you to go," he said bluntly. "Now."

"I have money," she protested.

"Don't matter. Get out."

She turned and left the store. The snorts of the shopkeeper stung like arrows in her spine. Her face burned with embarrassment. And now here came Sam, perking up at her elbow, inquisitive. He joggled the empty basket. "You get anythin'?"

75

"No, Sam," she said, choking on the words.

That was all there was to it. She had thought the ten dollars a hefty sum of money indeed. But it was expensive to be poor. And she had to live with that.

For a moment Eva had entertained visions of dressing up and tending to patients with the regal doctor's bag. But that was the white man's medicine. And she could have no part of it. Even if she wanted to.

"Better stick to what we know," she told Sam gloomily. "Let's go on home."

They walked down half the street before someone peeled out from the side of the building. He had his hat low at first, but the great height and staggering step gave him away instantly.

"Miss Eva," said the man.

She turned, startled. Sam grabbed her arm.

They were not that many white folks out, what with the encroaching rain; most were out to work, anyway. Still her eyes flung about for watchers. There were few.

"Oh- hello. Mr. Renard."

His appearance reminded her of the embarrassment in the shop. For a moment she wished he had never appeared. But he pushed up the brim of his hat with a knuckle and gave a friendly smile. The scarred half of his face seemed particularly dull. Her irritation melted.

"I believe I left my cane at your house," he said.

"Oh- I was gonna give it to John to return it for you. But I missed him on the way to work, I think..." Eva was mortified; she had forgotten, but she hoped he wouldn't think she had planned to keep it for herself!

"Don't bother John," he said. "I'm coming to fetch it myself."

"You mean- at my house?"

☐ "Of course. That's where I left it, isn't it?"

Eva's tongue was running ahead of her. The encounter with the shopkeeper had set her on edge. She calmed herself. "How did the medicine work for you?" she asked, resorting to familiar terrain.

"To tell you the truth," replied Renard, "It worked just fine."

"No pain?"

"Oh, the pain is there," he said with grim good humor, "But much less acute."

He turned to Sam, who walked rather stiffly next to his cousin. "You don't talk much, do you?"

"No sir," muttered Sam, mortified. Eva laid a hand

on his shoulder for comfort. She could not stop the young boy's unease towards the older white man, no more than she could stop the extreme ease she herself felt towards him.

"So where are you coming from?" asked Renard.

"The apothecary," said Eva.

"Oh?" the white man eyed her, and the empty basket. "You bought nothing?"

"No," she said lightly. "I decided not to."

"I see." He raised a dark eyebrow. "So, you mean to say, they would sell nothing to you?"

"That's right," said Eva, looking straight ahead. Renard stopped walking, and to be polite, so did she.

"What were you plannin' to buy?"

"Oh," she said, waving her hand, "I was lookin' at

some books."

"And the medical case," piped up Sam. Eva gave him A Look. She waited for the surprised expression to cross Mr. Mauricette's face: I didn't know negroes liked to read! But instead he looked annoyed.

"He wouldn't sell to you? You had money-"

"Yes," she said crisply, "I had my own money."

He still looked annoyed. Eva feared he might take it upon himself be one of those noble white folks who felt they had to Make A Scene. To prevent that, she hastily changed the subject. "You ain't limpin' nearly as much as you was," she said kindly.

"Thanks to you," he said. "A shame more people don't know of your talents. I bet you'd be a rich woman."

"I suppose," said Eva. She smiled. "I just tell myself I'm rich in other ways."

"I've been curious about something, Eva."

"Ask away."

"How is it that a poor woman with no formal training can heal what a European-educated doctor can't?"

"I didn't heal you," she said quickly. "Just helped with the pain."

Sam gave a quiet, opinionated snort.

"I haven't slept so well since I was a child," declared Renard. "My leg feels better than it has in months; my head is clear, I can walk with little pain. The humility is charming, my girl, but unnecessary."

My girl .

"I'm flattered," said Eva quietly. She made the mistake of glancing into his sloped cat-eyes. The expression there caught her off guard.

"Humor me," demanded Renard, leaning forward with interest. "How do you know the things you know?"

Eva shrugged. "How do the grass grow? Or the birds know when a storm comes? I don't know, Mr. Renard, how I knows the things I do. I just know. And what I wasn't taught, I taught myself."

"Remarkable," he said. "Do you read medical books?"

She looked at him saucily, as if to say, What do you think? Eva liked to read and so did most people in Rue Cher who knew how. As a result any book that came across her path was usually borrowed out and read and marked to tattered pieces. But she responded politely, "Never came an opportunity."

He nodded as if he understood. "When I was in France," he said, "I heard about a school of medicine. They allowed anyone in. Negroes, coloreds. They'd been doing it for centuries, you see, all the way back to the 18th century. None of that color nonsense, no segregation. You would never find that here, in Louisiana."

"No sir," she agreed, her interest piqued. "Not in this country, for sure. The French really do that?"

He nodded. "Funny, isn't it? Louisiana is the inheritor of the French in America. Decidedly so. But when it comes to the issue of color-" he waved his hand. "Never more American. The French think us barbarians. But some insist the only way to progress society is to keep the negroes out of any and everything. What do you think about that?"

"Well, I sure as hell don't like it," Eva blurted without thinking. Sam gave a strangled laugh at her side. And Renard laughed outright, so she continued.

"I can't but think about all the negroes who could have been somebody. I seen more fools among ten white folks than I seen among thirty negroes." She caught herself and quickly added, "Meanin' no offense. But don't nobody want to give us a chance. If we got some education, if they stopped runnin' off all the teachers that come 'round here, we might have a chance to lift ourselves up. That's all I'm sayin'."

She blushed and fell silent.

"Indeed," said Renard. He seemed to be looking at her differently now. This was the most she had ever spoken at once. He looked around her at Sam, who was burning with interest in the conversation, but trying not to look it.

"What do you think?" asked Renard.

"Me?" squeaked Sam.

"Sure."

"I think," he said, and licked his lips. Never had an adult included him in a conversation of this nature. "I think it uh, would be mighty nice to go to doctor school in France."

Eva hugged him 'round the shoulders affectionately. "You can do anythin' you put your heart to, Sammy."

Sam swallowed and nodded.

"There you have it," said Renard, satisfied. "Young ambition."

Eva broke into surprised laughter of her own. She couldn't wait to relay this conversation to the folks in Rue Cher. Renard Mauricette sure was a funny kind of white man.

Sam left the basket with Eva and hotfooted it away the moment they crossed the entrance of Rue Cher.

Renard then turned the conversation to even more serious things.

"There are some men who want this area away from the negroes," he said.

"White folks, you mean?"

"Yes."

"I own this land," said Eva. They had reached her house. It sat on the very edge of the village, in a pretty corner surrounded by all kinds of wildflowers and insects, the air punctuated by the beautiful trills of birds who, for the time being, had escaped the claws of Boots the cat. The gray sky seemed to bring out the bright green of the grass and the dogwood tree next to it, and the subtle grays of the stones Eva had lined up in front of the house. It would rain soon; Renard could smell it; his leg gave a painful twinge.

True to his word, Nelson had left a jar of honey out on Eva's step. No one had stolen it; her neighbors respected and feared her too much. She smiled when she saw the dried marigolds resting under it.

"I know," said Renard. He opened the gate for her. "I think it was my Granddaddy that sold it to your family."

"Not a lot of whites was sellin' to colored folks, in those days," she observed. Not a lot were selling to blacks in the present day, either.

She had just brought his cane out for him when a swollen cloud, purple and blue with heat and rain, burst over the village. Exclaiming, Eva rushed to pull her laundry from the line outside. Renard stood on the little porch and watched her. When she rushed back in, her arms laden and her cap soaked through, she was doubled over laughing.

"I must look a sight," she giggled. "I'm sorry, Mr. Renard." She piled the laundry on the chair and slicked a hand through her hair, the other hand on her waist. Oh, her smile. What a smile it was. It took up half her face, and seemed to light her eyes from within like two crystals.

Renard tore his eyes from her and eyed the sky, fiddling with the brim of his hat. "I hadn't expected rain."

"Set out here for a moment," said Eva, moving the laundry to her bed and bringing him the chair. He collapsed into it gratefully.

They watched the thunderheads approach in the distance, and Eva made coffee. She seemed to be always moving, always occupied with something. While she ground the beans a little tension line appeared between her eyebrows; she was thinking, always thinking. Renard had nothing to say about the chipped China she served the coffee in or its gritty taste, but he had a lot to say about other things. They talked for some time; Renard probing Eva about her practice, her medicines, and Eva asking Renard about the war.

The colored men that had left Rue Cher- and there were not very many- for the Great War had not returned. Or if they had, they came back maimed and soft in the head, husks of their former selves. Renard told Eva the negro men had been sent to the trenches first. Even in the army there had been segregation.

And somehow the conversation meandered back to Eva's visit to the apothecary. She had not intended to let it slip, but Renard was like a dog with a bone once he latched on to something.

" 'Gray's Anatomy'," he reflected. "Why, I believe we have that book at my house- an earlier edition, of course. I used it as a reference for drawing."

Eva held her breath. "Really?"

"Shall I bring it for you?"

"Oh-"

"On one condition."

"What's that?"

He rubbed his leg. "You make me some more of that medicine."

She smiled. "I need time to get everythin' I need."

"I've got nothing but time," he said. He smiled to himself, and dropped his eyes. She was startled at how long and sweeping the lashes were. So dark they seemed to give him an extraordinary beauty that didn't really belong on a man.

"Come back for it tomorrow," she said.

He sipped his coffee and eyed her. "And what if I want more the day after that?" he asked.

Eva felt a blush creep up her breasts. "Why, I expect you can come then too."

"Good," he murmured. "I'd like that."

Renard left as soon as the rain abated, with promises to bring the book for Eva and to stop by soon. Eva wondered how Sam could have said the man had a curse on him.

He walked upright now, harmless and mannish. He splashed right through the puddles in his gentleman's boots, the water and grass stalks eddying from his path. Eva stood on her porch and watched his heavy gait with a doctor's eye. He limped less, and didn't use the cane.

He was a mystery to her, not in the usual way that white folks were mysterious, but in the way that animals were mysterious, and the weather, and the behavior of all living things. She wanted to know more about him. From Renard she had not yet felt that sense of entitlement towards her that most men seemed to have.

So it was thoughts of Renard Mauricette that haunted Eva's mind as she set out in the dimming twilight to gather mistletoe.

CHAPTER THREE

A tall woman rode a horse into Rue Cher. Her hair, black as a pitch lake, hung in a loose braid to her waist. She rode loosely too, with the ease of a Comanche warrior. Yet the woman was not Comanche (nor was she fully white, though few would dare challenge that).

On every finger a ring burned. Jasper, rubies, sapphires, emeralds. The jasper matched the red horse's coat. The emeralds matched her eyes. Green eyes, from her father.

This woman was of course Amelie Mordant. Or Amelie Mauricette, if you were inclined to be technical. Though no one called her that. In these parts she would always be a Mordant, of the old blood of France.

She rode into Rue Cher past the black men stooping over the fields, past the black women stooping over their washing, past the black children stooping over games of jacks. The folk stared but found they could not stare for long. She hurt to look at, like an open wound.

Eventually the red horse stopped in front of a small cabin with lots of flowers and a dogwood tree in the front. A shiver fluttered up Amelie Mordant's spine. Her rings grew cold.

"Interestin'," she murmured, "very interestin'."

She clicked her tongue, the horse moved on.

The Mauricettes called a family meeting. Renard had to be coaxed from his study by his little sister Fiona. Once he entered the parlor it became clear he'd been tricked; his uncle, mother, sisters and father-in-law had arranged themselves in a tight semi-circle facing a single chair, where he was to sit.

An interrogation.

"Dear," began his mother, "Please have a seat."

Renard sat. His eyes flitted around the room. Betty the maid, a dark woman in a servant's frock, laid out a plate of scones. Her eyes flicked knowingly up to Renard's. And then he perceived what this meeting was really about.

"Long time no see, boy," rumbled Louis Mordant.

"Indeed," said Renard. His leg began to throb. He rubbed it so he wouldn't clench his fists.

"I suppose we ought to get right into it," twittered his

mother. She reached for a scone and spoke between nibbling bites. "We heard you've been going down to the village."

"I have," said Renard immediately, his temper flaring to the surface. "Would you like a written account of what I've been doing, mother? Should I have brought an escort? An armed guard?"

"Don't be like this," hissed Madame Mauricette. "You've brought enough shame on this family, Renard-"

"We are so worried about you," said Fiona.

Louis Mordant nodded. His beady green eyes gleamed. He had another motive for being here, but enjoyed watching the uppity Monsieur Mauricette taken down a peg or two.

"I am a grown man," Renard reminded them acidly, "Not a simpering boy. I go where I please."

"Fraternizing with negroes!" screeched his mother, so loud Betty jumped and spilled the tea she'd been pouring. Madame aimed a kick at Betty's shin, which the girl dodged nimbly.

"I will 'fraternize' with whomever I please," said Renard through his teeth. He couldn't help feeling like a cornered schoolboy trying to talk his way out of a beating.

"Son," intoned Louis Mordant, "Please be reasonable. Your mother is right. It's an affront to common decency, a white man of good family, socializing with negro women. What the devil has gotten into you? May I remind you, Renard, that you have a wife. My daughter Amelie-"

At the mention of Amelie's name all Renard's composure shattered.

"Don't patronize me, Monsieur. These negro women you speak of are more constant than your well-bred cow of a daughter," he spat.

"How dare you!" roared Louis.

Renard staggered to his feet. The pain in his leg was blinding. "I do dare," he said. "If she really has come back here, I don't want her. In fact, I mean to go to the courts tomorrow and get my divorce. Now get out of my house."

"You worm," spat Louis. He had gone a curdled white. Divorce, in the staunch Catholic Louisiana society, would bring untold shame on his daughter.

"My daughter doesn't deserve a blighted cripple!"

"A shame you didn't think of that sooner," said Renard. His voice was razor sharp. "It was the fortune, not the woman, I married when I took Amelie's hand. Now I say to hell with both. I don't give a damn about your daughter or your money."

"She has a son- your son-" Madame Mauricette quacked, trying, in her womanish way, to appeal to some baser sensitivity.

Renard's laughter rang through the parlor horribly. Betty had shrunk away into the corner, her eyes round as silver dollars and glittering with interest. No doubt she would be carrying news of this quarrel all the way to Rue Cher before the day was out.

"I would like to know how I fathered a child a continent away in the French trenches, with half my body in a plaster cast."

He turned to leave. Fiona was weeping pettishly into a scrap of lace. His mother was deciding if she ought to brain her son with the glass decanter. Louis Mordant got to his feet.

"On behalf of your mother and good society," he declared, "I must warn you, you insolent boy. If you continue to reject your natural wife and son, if you continue your dalliances with the niggers, there will be hell to pay."

"I have seen hell already," said Renard. "And I daresay you are not one to judge me for who I choose to love. You, monsieur, who has raped half the negro maids in his service." He lurched through the door and slammed it.

Determination was stamped across his face. He stumbled up the staircase, nearly having to walk on all fours. His bones burned inside him like hot metal splinters. Agony, blinding agony. Of course, he'd forgotten to apply Eva's ointment the night before. Now the pain had gone beyond the power of basic folk remedies. He needed morphine, and he needed it now.

Breathing hard, Renard shuffled into the study that had once belonged to Gaspard Mauricette. He could hear his mother's aggrieved cries echoing through the house. They filled him with resolve. He would not take morphine. He would not become what they wanted him to be.

The marriage license and certificate were buried under some other paperwork in a drawer. Renard pounced on them and tucked them away in his coat. He would walk to the courthouse if he had to. He would crawl. And then he would return every penny of Amelie Mordant's dowry, and divorce the bitch once and for all. Not necessarily in that order.

Downstairs Madame Mauricette complained long and loudly to Monsieur Mordant. The gentleman tried to put her at ease.

"Something will be done, Madame. The boy is young."

"Not that young," said Madame bitterly. "He is almost twenty-four."

"He has had a traumatic experience," said Louis. "Perhaps the war has addled his head. Yes, I have heard of many such cases. Fine young men return home and take up with the worst of vagabonds, in some effort to attain the sense of comradeship they lost on the battlefield. Some even become opium addicts-"

Madame Mauricette let out a scandalized shriek.

"Not to say Renard is one," amended Louis. "But you must be vigilant. You must prevent him from going to Rue Cher. Offer him encouraging alternatives."

"And what of Amelie?" said Madame. "Those things he said about her- and she is such a good girl! I would not believe it for an instant, Monsieur, I assure you..."

"Let me worry about Renard," said Louis, and there was something of the wolf in his smile. "And I will find out what will be done about Amelie."

A meeting of another kind was happening on Eva

LaLaurie's porch. It was Sunday, and church was out.

Some people brought lunch- candied yams, roast fowl, greens. A couple men went out to try to catch a baby gator. The afternoon bore down, a mouth-watering smell rose up from Eva's yard, and the liquor passed freely.

The conversation struck upon familiar, comfortable subjects: what the pastor's wife was wearing, what the crop yield was going to look like, what Beamer Joe, the Rue Cher guitarist who'd gone to strike his fortune in New Orleans jazz parlors, was up to.

But the talk could not stay away from the community's most pressing issue for long.

"Now, I don't get it," said Trout Jenkins. "I don't get what these white folks want."

"Money," said Mitch Davis.

"Land," suggested Nelson.

"It don't have to be that," said Tom Shanter, his loud voice carrying. "Whatever black folks want, the white folks want too. You could be walkin' past 'em wid nothin but a 'possum tail and a walnut in your pocket, and some cracker would say, 'what's that you got? give it here, nigger.' "

They cackled. A couple of the women, who stood back talking with Eva, glared disapprovingly.

"That man's too dumb to spit," said Sarie Jules. She spooned some crawfish from the pot and heaped it on her plate. Tom heard her and leaned back in his chair merrily. "What's that, Sarie?"

Sarie Jules raised her voice. "I said whatever your mouth is throwin', your ass better know how to catch it."

That broke them all up again.

"Two nights ago a cracker comes knockin' on my

door," said Tom, once the laughter died. "He says, 'how much you want for this land?' "

"Short fella?" asked Mitch Davis. "Ugly coat?"

"Yep. Face like a sick frog, too. He says, 'how much you want for this land, nigger?' So I says, 'more than what your mama gave you, sir.' He turns dark as a plum and starts hollerin' about disrespect and he'll have some folks over here to string me from the rafters."

The company fell quiet. Threats of lynching were serious- and they all knew Tom and his runaway mouth had had their fair share of close calls.

"What you say?" said Esau.

"Well then I played stupid, and I ran him some story 'bout how I didn't want to sell 'cause my grandmomma was buried there, and I wore him down 'till he left. He said he'd be back, though. But I'm ready for 'im. Nobody's gonna take what's mine."

"Don't do nothin' foolish, Tom," put in Bess Jules, in her small voice.

"Don't you worry," said Tom. "Ain't never seen more chicken white folks in my born days than what they got here in Rue Cher. They afraid of they own shadows."

It turned out several folks had been visited by the mysterious pair of white men. They'd shooed them away by playing stupid or making thinly-veiled threats. But the seed had been planted and all of them, even Tom, were worried. Whatever tenuous peace agreement there was between them and the white folks was being threatened. Someone had put eyes on their land- and they would just have to deal with it.

"I don't know what's so special about this place," said Esau, shaking his head.

But they knew- they all knew. What made Rue Cher special was their community. Like a family, each one interconnected by something more powerful than skin. Their bond with each other ran as deep as the roots of the willow trees.

Once all the visitors left, Eva got out her anatomy book and started studying.

The book was fascinating. She hadn't known there were so many parts to the human body, each with a different name, many she had to sound aloud to pronounce. Some of the illustrations were frighteningly detailed.

Eva had seen the white men doing their doctoring from a distance. They came into Rue Cher- the white section, of course- with black bags and long coats, looking very important, looking very sinister. Eva had no pretensions of wanting to be a doctor like that- they wouldn't let her study medicine anyway, as a woman, even if she wasn't black. Perhaps a nurse might be better suited.

If she could, in any way, make people feel better...why, she would find a way to do it, and she would study what she needed. The white folks might bar her from their schools, on account of her race and gender.

Eva had never heard of female doctors- and certainly not black female doctors. Yet they existed. Had she known of their existence, her thoughts might have taken a more optimistic turn.

As she sat there reading, enjoying the lazy heat of the Sunday afternoon, she heard a familiar hailing from her gate. She closed the book and went to look. Of course it was Renard.

Her heart gave a quick jump. A traitorous leap. She pressed her hands to her chest and stilled her nerves. What was wrong with her?

"Miss Eva?" he called.

She was not home. She was busy. She was just

leaving. A hundred excuses jumped into Eva's head, and she couldn't say why, but she went out and let him in anyway.

"Why, Mister Renard," she smiled tensely. "I didn't expect you today."

Every time this particular white gentleman came to her cabin, he found some reason to stay longer and longer. Mostly they just got to talking. Eva found she liked his company. He was quite funny, in a biting, sarcastic way not too different from her cousin Esau or Tom Shanter. So she couldn't explain the sudden urge she had today to request he leave and shut the door in his face.

"Apologies," said Renard, and immediately she detected something was wrong. Some dark temper had clouded his brow. Unease stamped itself all over his face; his eyes darted around, looking everywhere but into hers.

"I have your payment," he said heavily.

"Oh." Eva stared. "For what?"

He dragged his left leg behind him when he ducked through the door- he had not brought his cane. From his pockets he drew another ten dollars and set it on her table.

"No," she said firmly, "This is too much." She gathered the money and pushed it towards him.

"I decide if it's too much. Take it."

What arrogance! Eva bristled. "Mr. Renard, I don't take charity. Not from white folks."

He glared at her. "I'm paying you for a service, damn it."

"But I haven't done anything."

"Why do you think I'm here?" he snapped.

She sighed in irritation and shut the door behind him. "You in pain?"

Unable to bear it any longer, Renard collapsed in her single chair. His body seemed to crumple around the wounded leg, which stuck out stiffly on the footrest in front of him. "Yes," he said into his hands.

A cold feeling went through Eva. A feeling like she was being watched from inside her own house. She shuddered violently. Renard's hands still cupped his face. She could hear his labored breathing from across the room. He was in pain so great, and he had dragged himself here to see her.

She had a sudden urge to fling herself at his feet and kiss him, tell him it would be alright. Even in the throes of pain, his countenance marred by a steady flush up his throat and cheeks, Renard appeared a very handsome man. His big hands clenched and unclenched over his thighs.

"I'm in agony," murmured Renard. "I need you to

help me."

"Sure thing," she murmured. "I'll get you better."

Once, when she was small, Eva's grandmother had owned a dog.

Thorn: a great shaggy beast folks said was mixed with coyote or wolf. Though Nanny said it was bad to get close to animals, he had seemed the strongest dog in the world, and she had been attached to him- as all children are attached to proud and noble things. One day Thorn ate something bad and got sick. Nanny said the white folks across the river had poisoned him. He lay in a crumpled heap on the step. Pink foam leaked from his muzzle. He wouldn't even take Nanny's medicine. So Nanny fetched Nelson's gun and put him down.

Renard Mauricette reminded Eva of Thorn. A proud, willful, defeated creature. A lonely man. And a feeling of great pity overcame her. She rushed to his side impulsively and put her arms around him.

"I'll get you better," she promised. "You don't worry 'bout it."

He smelled wonderful. Like cloves and leather and smooth ivory soap...the stubble on his jaw scratched her cheek. Realizing she was out of place she tried to pull away, but he gripped her arm. His head tipped back and his gaze locked with hers. She swallowed.

"There's more than one way you can help me."

She froze for a dizzying second. In the shifting light his eyes seemed inhuman, feline, calculating. But then he frowned and the spell was broken. He reached his other hand up to pluck a delicate eyelash from her cheek.

"Help you how?" she said.

He didn't answer. He just looked at her.

"I can make you somethin' else," she whispered. "Just

wait right here."

But she didn't move, and neither did he. His eyes seemed to be probing at her with a question. She pulled away.

"You know," he said huskily, "I don't really know why I came here. I should have sent John for morphine."

"If it's morphine you want, that I don't have," said Eva.

"I don't want morphine, though, truly. I want this pain gone."

"Then cut off your leg," said Eva. She had meant it as a joke. It didn't come out like one.

He rolled his eyes. "Yes."

"Listen, Mr. Renard-"

"By the blood of Jesus. Please stop saying that."

"Sayin' what?"

"Renard. Please just call me Renard. I'm your patient, not your employer."

Eva stepped back, her annoyance mounting. The strange feeling of the moment was gone. She didn't know who Renard Mauricette thought he was, to two-step into her house and snap at her like a kicked dog. He could take his ten dollars and stick it where the sun didn't shine.

"Listen-" she began, about to tell him as much. But then he did the unthinkable- he apologized.

"I'm sorry," he murmured. He rubbed his face and got to his feet. "Forgive me." He stepped outside.

Not once in her life had she heard a white person apologize for anything. And that gave her pause.

She looked at the long slope of his back as he leaned against her porch railing. Renard was not like any other white person she had met. It was a little crazy. He didn't insist on all that scraping and begging that even her white customers from over the river seemed to demand in some way or form. He never raised his voice and he always said exactly what was on his mind. What you saw with Renard Mauricette was what you got.

Shaking her head, she turned to make more of the medicine. Not that she expected it to help- It seemed Renard needed something stronger.

She finished up and stepped outside to hand it to him. Renard had lit a cigarette. The smoke formed around his head like a noxious halo. His left hand lay clenched on his thigh.

The way he presented himself had always fascinated Eva. He dressed like the other white gentry- but with none of the frills and arrogant severity. The ring he'd had on the first day she met him was gone. Renard's clothes were always simple and well-made. Often rumpled. He never remained still for long.

He was also a good listener. None of the other folks in Rue Cher trusted him, but Eva found he had wormed his way into her inner confidence without her knowing it. White or no, she considered Renard a friend. A friend you kept at arm's length was still a friend.

She arranged her skirts and sat next to him. He offered her a new cigarette but, feeling bold, she plucked the one he held between his lips and took a quick pull of her own.

"You got somethin' on your spirit," she said, handing it back to him.

"I don't aim to make my problems yours."

"Then don't."

"Can I trust you with what's on my 'spirit'?"

"That's up to you," said Eva. "Trust is give and take. I trust you to let you into my place when it's just the two of us. I trust you with the knowin' of my family and my medicine. But it seems you got more to hide than I do, so I can see why your trust is harder won."

"My family found out I was coming here," he said. "They weren't happy. Some little spies have their eye on you, I think. But you know something? I don't particularly care. I do as I please."

"I don't look for trouble," said Eva nervously. The last thing she wanted was to get the attention of any white folks. "And besides, we're not doin' anythin'...inappropriate." He looked at her suddenly, sharply. She flushed and looked away.

"Right," he said softly. The cigarette burned itself to a stub when he dropped it. He watched it die.

"No one's going to do anything to you," he said, so

firmly she believed him. "But enough. I am so curious about you, Little Miss LaLaurie. Tell me something about yourself."

"Myself?"

"Yes. What troubles you, Eva?"

Eva blinked. "I don't got nothin' troublin' me, Renard," she said. "I get by just fine. I got a roof over my head. I got food on my table. I got a family."

He looked at her critically. "You have no complaints?"

White folks tryin' to take our land, she thought. Somebody comin' after me leavin' ill-wishes on my door. But even these things seemed far away, distant problems for another time. Yes, she was happy.

"No," she said. "All my complaints is for other people. I want what's best for the folks here. I get by with what I have- and I got more than most."

"You humble me," he murmured. "Some days I feel like I don't want to keep going on. It all seems so miserable and pointless. But you're right- I have more than most. That's enough, I think, to live on."

"You'll get better," she told him. "Your mind got to be strong, so your body can be stronger. Don't forget that."

A soft wind picked up and ruffled through his hair. Eva's brown hand lay next to his fist. He looked at her hand and his fist clenched and unclenched, as if he wanted to touch it.

"You know what my favorite thing about August is?" murmured Renard. He stared out at her garden. The spilling flowers, the vines snaking up old furniture and abandoned woodpiles. The steady march of fire ants around a frog carcass near the fencepost. A bed of roses winding up the fence itself, wild and thorny, carelessly beautiful. The smell of pinks hung in the air. They could hear the hum of bees.

"No," she said softly.

"Every living thing is most beautiful in August. It's almost as if- as if they don't know about the cold. They keep on anyway, puttin' out that beauty. And for what? I wonder."

"I guess that is just life," said Eva. "We're never gonna be more beautiful than we are now. Every moment, we losin' time. But that's how it's 'posed to be. We 'posed to die, so somethin' more beautiful can come after."

"You have a philosophical mind."

"Ain't philosophy," Eva teased. "That's just real science."

"Science, eh? And what do you know about science?"

"I know enough," she said. "Just ask your leg."

"You do," he conceded, laughing. "You know, Eva. I'd like to compare you with one of the so-called 'learned' doctors. How can you do what they can't?"

"I do what I'm taught," she said simply. "And they be doin' the same."

"But who is your teacher now?" he said. "You didn't learn all of what you know from one person, surely."

He had asked that question once before. "Experience was my teacher," she said. She gestured to the garden, the trees, the forest. "All I know comes from that. The world."

"Fascinating."

"I ain't the best, but I learn from what I see, not what people tell me to see."

"But there is only one truth, no? In medicine, I mean. There is a way to cure and a way to hurt."

"No," said Eva, shaking her head. "I don't b'lieve that. It ain't what I was taught. That's what you white folks don't get. All your book learnin' only gonna get you so far. Y'all want to put everythin' in a corner with a pretty little name over it. 'Whites' over here. 'Negroes' over there. And then you find it ain't as simple as all that, so what do you do? You go on makin' smaller names and smaller corners. Corners in corners."

"So there's no objective truth, not even in medicine?"

"Maybe there is. I'm just sayin' truth and medicine change all the time, dependin' on who or what is standin' in front of you. One man's medicine is another's poison."

"Revolutionary."

"That's right. Too much focusin' on the trees an' you gonna miss the whole forest. But you can't look at a single tree and think all other trees are just like it. It's about balancin' what you know to be true, and what is standin' right before your eyes."

"So what makes you able to balance that? What makes your medicine special?"

She laughed. "What I got is in here," she replied, tapping her forehead. "Is same as what's out there. It's instinct. It's soul. You either got it or you don't."

He was looking at her intently. "You know," he said, "Sometimes when you speak, I get the feeling I should be writing it all down."

"Maybe you ought to," said Eva, smiling. She almost wished he would look away. He was sitting too close to her; she could count the very faint freckles on his nose, each long, dark eyelash...

"What kind of things you paint?" she asked him, grasping for a new subject.

"Anything," he said. "Mostly landscapes."

"You ever paint people?"

"Sometimes," he said smoothly. "Only the ones I love."

He reached for her arm and pulled her to him roughly. She didn't resist. Her hands came up around his shoulders. His hands circled around her waist and drew her to his chest. His lips teased over hers, unassuming, gentle, firm.

He had kissed her because he felt like it, he had kissed her because he saw her as an angel, he had kissed her for a hundred reasons. And what happened? The earth didn't open up and swallow them. The sun didn't fall from the sky. It was the most natural thing in the world to sit there and kiss Eva LaLaurie. And she did not pull away, but kissed him back with a fervor and passion he would not have anticipated.

Renard was lost.

He pulled her on top of him. His black curls spread

out behind his head like a devil's halo. They fell backwards on the porch. Through the fabric of her simple dress Renard got a feel for the shape of her breasts. They thrust out towards him; his large rough hands molded and weighed them. Eva whimpered into his mouth. He ground his good leg up to press against her dress and the fork of her legs where the source of her heat and passion flowered. Her eyes flicked up to his.

Did she know? Did she know that she had bewitched him so completely?

They checked themselves; they were sprawled out against each other in full view of anyone who walked by. Time to be sensible. They ducked back inside, straightening themselves.

"Renard," Eva began, "I don't think-"

But he wasn't listening; he seized her arm again and pulled her to him roughly. His lips came down over hers. One hand bracing on the closed door, the other gripping Eva's bottom and holding her firmly against him, he explored the sweet wet heat of her mouth with his tongue. Eva melted in his embrace. Her hands slid over his chest, hovering at his stomach, afraid to go any lower...

"I don't know anythin'," she said.

"I'll show you what to do," he murmured.

They fell atop Eva's pallet. Her curiosity seemed to mirror his. They said almost nothing to each other; they wanted to see how far the other would go.

Renard ruched Eva's dress up to her waist. His fingers left impressions in the silky-smooth skin of her thighs. She was brown, all brown, and pink at the middle. Holding both thighs strongly between his hands, Renard parted her and delved into the glistening flower with his tongue. Eva arched under him, her gasp shooting to the ceiling. A feeling grew inside her...a sensation.

It was magic, a bloom of exhilarating rapture that seized hold of her and made her press against him. A storm of pleasure bore her up against him, mingling their breaths, their pants, and Eva's cries in a symphony that seemed to shake the foundations of the house. Every moment spun itself into a dizzying web, binding her closer, closer, to a forbidden desire she could not name...

He tongued the bud of her clit expertly and he released her thighs to slide two fingers into her. She came shaking in his hands like she would fall apart. Her hands dug into his broad shoulders. She didn't know if she could take any more. Still, he caressed her. If not with his hands then with his tongue. He slid from the folds of her pussy up the planes of her stomach, his hands still exploring. And his mouth met hers again. She could taste herself on him.

When he rose up over her, Eva expected his hands to reach for his belt, unleash the sizeable bulge stirring under the fabric of his pants and claim her right there on the floor.

But he did not. He instead pulled her dress down and smoothed it over her knees. His curly hair was disheveled. Only the bursts of their strained breathing could be heard. Then he got to his feet and helped her up.

"Not like this," was all he said. He looked at her and touched her cheek, and then his hand grabbed her chin fiercely and he jerked her towards him again. This time he stepped her into the wall of the house and kissed her soundly. If Eva was water, Renard was pure fire. His mouth burned against hers.

Disoriented, her knees shaking, Eva saw him out the door.

"A fine house you have, dear." The voice came low as a cat's purr, and was unmistakably a white woman's. Eva raised her head from her flowerbed.

"Good afternoon," she said cautiously.

The woman was leaning up against her gate. Even with the sun in her eyes (and her eyesight not what it used to be) Eva could see her quite clearly. She had a kind of dark white skin, and very long black hair. She wore a lot of jewelry.

Boots the cat gave a hiss and vanished behind the house.

"Are you Eva?" said the woman.

"Yes," said Eva. Instinct told her to be cautious. She did not like this woman's tone. "Can I help you, Ma'am?"

"My name is Amelie," said the woman. "Amelie Mauricette. My father is Louis Mordant. I live the parish over."

Eva's eyebrows shot up her forehead. Of course she had heard of the Mordants- they owned half the state, practically- but she didn't know what the hell one of their own was doing here, leaning over her fencepost.

And she couldn't miss that the lady had styled herself Mauricette. Renard's name.

"Can I help you, Ma'am?" Eva repeated.

"Oh, certainly." The woman's tone was gently mocking. If housecats could speak, they would sound like her. "I'll get right to it," said the woman. "I know you've been seeing Renard."

Alarm bells tolled in Eva's head. She drew herself up. "Renard Mauricette?" she tweeted. Play dumb. It's what she expects.

"Yes, girl. Renard Mauricette."

"I tend to him, yes. Like I do lots of people. I'm his doctor."

The woman twisted a ring on her finger. "Tend to , that's a sweet way to put it. Do you know that he is married?"

"Yes," Eva lied smoothly. "I did know that."

Inside she was choking. Of all the things she had expected, it hadn't been this. Renard did not seem the type. But of course, no man ever did! Married!? she thought. Devil strike me down!

The woman seemed to be enjoying herself. She licked her lips with a pert red tongue. "Yes. Renard is my husband. I'm his lawful wife."

"I wish you many blessings," said Eva tersely.

At that moment Sam came ambling down the path, barefoot, his fishing pole balancing on his shoulder and a bucket in hand. He and his whistling stopped dead at the sight of the white woman. His dark skin flushed. Dropping his fishing pole, he ducked his head and slid over Eva's fence.

The change on the woman's face was immediate. She watched him with open disgust.

"I hate the sight of these pickaninnies," she spat. "You, boy. Come here."

Sam shot a glance at Eva.

"Come here," the woman repeated sharply. Sam went.

"What's your name?" said Amelie.

"Sam."

"Speak to me properly. What are you doing?"

"Goin' fishin', Ma'am," mumbled Sam.

Amelie's hand shot out and gripped the boy's chin.

Her other hand fisted in his hair; he yelped in surprise. Eva started forward, but as soon as Sam's discolored eyes met the white woman's, she let go of him immediately. Her hand withdrew as if he'd burned her. She wiped it on her skirts.

"What's wrong with your eyes, boy?" she said.

"Nothin'," said Sam. His hands and voice began to tremble. With rage, and not with fear. "I was borned this way. Ma'am."

Eva pulled her little cousin back from the woman and stepped between them. "Better tell me what I can help you with so you can go along your way."

The woman tossed her oily rope of hair. Her eyes sparkled. "I never took no sass from a nigger woman, and I won't start now."

Eva's large eyes narrowed to slits. "You got no fight with me."

"Renard is my husband," repeated Amelie. "If I find you've been openin' your pocketbook for him, or any white man, I'll be back with men of my own. And we'll burn this house to bare cinders. With you inside it."

"Don't you threaten her!" cried Sam bravely.

"Excuse me?" barked the woman.

"No need for that," said Eva calmly, twisting her hand in Sam's shirt. "Mr. Mauricette won't be back here again. I don't want no trouble under my roof."

"He better not be back here. And I'll have ways of knowing if he is. I make myself clear, girl?"

"Clear as day, Ma'am," said Eva. The memory of Renard's kiss burned on her lips. The kiss that had been a lie. Of course he would be married to this- this creature. She had been a fool.

Amelie straightened up and flicked open her fan.

"Good afternoon, then."

The white woman strolled back down the path. Eva watched her mount a great red horse and turn towards the road that wound uphill towards the Mauricette house.

Sam spat in the dust she left.

"Wicked bitch," said Eva. "Did she hurt you, Sammy?"

"Naw," said the boy, rubbing his head. He glanced at Eva. "I'd be more worried if I was you."

"Aw, she ain't gonna do nothin'," snorted Eva.

"She ain't right," Sam persisted. "She was all wrong. She got somethin' bad about her. Somethin' dark. Like she ain't a full person."

"What you talkin'bout? Of course she's a full person. Just an old bitter demon. Like the rest of 'em."

"She's a witch," declared Sam, lowering his voice as if Amelie Mordant might appear from under Eva's step any moment. "I can feel it on her."

"A white gal?" Eva almost laughed. "I never heard such a thing. You sure?"

"She ain't white, then," Sam persisted. "I done told you to put somethin' on the house after you let that Mauricette in. Now you got witches runnin' all over the place."

"I'll be fine," said Eva, steadying herself on the fencepost. "Someone left a little ill-wish on my door, is all..."

"Nelson told me about that."

"Nelson a fool. I'll be fine, Sammy. Don't you worry 'bout it."

"You too stubborn," Sam said with some brass in his

voice. Eva realized, with dim shock, that her cousin was angry with her. "You did never listen. Put somethin' on the house, Eva. If it ain't already too late."

"Oh, Sam."

He broke off from her hug and patted down his clothes like he was looking for something.

"I meant to give you this, but I f'got the last time."

He reached into his pocket and pulled out a little pouch. The pouch dangled at the end of a leather rope that looked a lot like an old shoelace.

"What's this?"

"Somethin' Ma Delphine taught me," he said. Ma Delphine had been his grandmother, and a rumored conjure woman. The folk of Rue Cher didn't hold too well with magic. Some might say what Eva did was a kind of magic, but of course they would always agree that what she did was different. Her stuff wasn't really spells. It was medicine.

Sam looked at Eva quickly to see if she would disapprove. But Eva was open-minded to most things of this nature. She opened the bag. Inside were three of Sam's hairs, a small hermit crab shell, and a feather.

"If you needin' me," said Sam, pointing in the bag, "You just got to knot one of them hairs."

The folk believed hair was a powerful thing. You couldn't leave your old hairs around 'cause a bird would make a nest of it. You couldn't let anyone get a piece of your hair, 'cause they might take it to a witch and she might put a Working on you. All hair had to be swept up and burned the second it fell from your head.

Sam's gift was precious, but dangerous. He had given her a piece of himself. Eva closed the bag and tied the lace around her neck.

"Don't take it off," he warned. "Nanny said if you take it off it's gonna lose the power."

He looked at her earnestly with those mismatched eyes. Eva felt a surge of love for her little cousin. "You too young to be fussin' after me like that. You know I'll be alright." But she pulled him to her- he struggled to break free, aw, shucks Eva- and kissed his head anyway. "Come inside for some tea?"

"Momma wants me to catch a chubsucker for dinner. 'Gotta get it while the light's good."

"If you see that white woman again, you best just run in the other direction. She's up to no good."

"Don't got to tell me twice."

He allowed her to give him another kiss. Then he picked up his fishing rod and bucket and ambled down to the river.

Eva watched her little cousin go. He was a good soul.

One day he would be a fine man and make some woman really happy. But she worried about him living in a place like this. A black woman could always get a maid's job here, save up and try to edge a way forward for her children. But black men had few options to rise above their station. No man in Louisiana would hire a black man if they could get a white or an Irish to do the job. It was a sorry fact.

Sam couldn't spend the rest of his days fishing in the river, playing spades and tilling the earth. Nothing was wrong with honest labor, of course, but he had to have some other options. Smart as he was, surely the Lord had destined him for something greater.

As for herself, well, her life course had been set. Eva would probably stay in Rue Cher for the rest of her life. She'd been fated to be the healer. But Sam deserved more. She touched the little bag at her throat and blinked back tears. If only she could do more for those she loved most.

The next day Renard Mauricette went to the courthouse and filed for divorce.

The next day Eva LaLaurie made seven house calls over a sudden outbreak of chicken pox.

The next day Tom Shanter took the usual left turn down the Magru Road to get to his house, which he shared with his common-law wife and two stepdaughters. And he stopped dead in his tracks, because there were three white men standing outside this house. One of them had a torch. One of them had a small stack of papers. The other one had a rifle.

"Took you long enough, nigger," said Charles St. Joseph, who held the papers.

Tom walked up to the gate slowly. He walked as if through jelly.

"What y'all want?" he said softly. Their eyes gleamed like snakes' eyes. Cold, inhuman.

"I done told you two weeks ago what I wanted," snarled St. Joseph. He shook the papers at Tom. "Your sister gave me these. These is your land papers."

"I know what they are," said Tom, his voice still soft. He moved very slowly and carefully towards them. When faced with a wild animal, best be quiet and still as possible.

"Smart boy," laughed Rifle.

Tom looked around for help. The cabin sat comfortably on the perimeter of Rue Cher. Tom owned one of the largest pieces of property in the village, which meant he had a very isolated position. The only other folks that shared the perimeter with him were Eva LaLaurie, who would be of no help, and Nelson the Indian, who was never home. He looked around anyway for anyone, some miracle, that could help.

On the next hill over a white woman on a red horse stood watch over the proceedings. She and the horse stood still as trees. As statues. There was a man, also mounted, standing with her.

"Bet you thought you'd have us pinned down before we could get to you," snarled Charles St. Joseph. Tom's eyes focused back to the present.

"I didn't think nothing," said Tom slowly. He was at a loss for what to do. The only recourse would be to try to talk them out of burning down the house and into just giving him a beating.

No matter what, though, he wasn't going to sell his land. That was for damn certain.

"I'm sorry," said Tom, the words tasting like poison. "I misspoke last time. My head wasn't on right. Maybe we can all sit down and talk like men."

From behind his house he caught a tiny, dark figure in a yellow dress sprinting away in the opposite direction. His breath whistled out.

Anastasie, his stepdaughter, had probably gotten out through the hole behind the stove...she was the only one small enough to fit. Tom prayed for a miracle.

"You ain't a man," said Charles. "That's for sure."

"Eyes over here, boy," snarled Torch.

"Sign these," said Charles St. Joseph. "And make it quick."

"I ain't know how to write," lied Tom, stalling for time. Rifle cracked him across the face with the rifle. He didn't hit hard, but Tom's bad front tooth went flying from his mouth. Blood seeped over his lips and sank into the earth, which he was suddenly no longer standing on, but grasping between his fists. He didn't even remember falling.

"Lyin' coon," said St. Joseph. "I seen you down over the river at the general store. I seen you write. Don't make me ask again."

Tom needed more time.

"I don't know!" he shrieked, so loud they jumped. If he couldn't play dumb, he'd play crazy. He beat his hands against his chest. "Oh Lord! I don't know - I forgot-"

The men were not amused. "You want us to burn 'em up?" roared St. Joseph. He kicked Tom viciously in the ribs.

"Get up!"

They dragged him to his feet and began to beat him. Tom was not a small man. In an even fight he could have handled all three of them. But any movement to defend himself, and Rifle would plant an ounce of lead in his stomach.

He didn't have to take their punches long, and in the process of rolling around and hollering he bumped into Torch, who stumbled over his own flat feet and dropped the burning wood. It rolled merrily away from them. Madder than ever, all three started wailing on Tom for good. With every blow he bellowed and screamed as loud as he could, and for once his loud, carrying lungs would be his saving grace.

"Shut up!" bawled Charles St. Joseph.

But for once Tom's talented lungs would be his saving grace. More than his stepdaughter's swiftness, his cries carried news of what was happening over the ridge and help was soon on the way. Above Tom's screams, an exaggerated, blood-curdling whoop sounded from the trees. And there came Nelson, his blue hat flying off his head, running fast as a deer, with another man behind him. The white men stared in bare shock before Rifle remembered he was armed. He roared and raised the gun, but Nelson was faster. And his gun, which had been his son's army issue in the war, was the superior.

The Indian planted his feet and fired. The shot took Rifle's hat clean off his head. The next shot, from Esau LaLaurie, went wide and punched through Tom Shanter's closed window.

"Watch where you're firin', you damned jackass!" Tom bellowed.

"Shoot him!" screamed Charles St. Joseph to his companion. "What's the matter with you?"

But then Nelson had reloaded, and the shots burst on the ground in front of the white men's feet with astonishing precision. The prisoners in the house screamed, sure that Tom was being killed.

"Bleedin' Jesus, it's a sharpshooter," said Rifle, turning to run.

"You got a gun too, you yellow bastard!" barked Charles. To no avail. Knowing they were beaten, the men fled.

Tom let his head fall back to the earth. The woman on the hill was gone.

Nelson and Esau rushed over.

"Y'all is dead men," groaned Tom through a bubbly mouthful of blood. He clutched his liver. Surely the bastards hadn't busted it up that bad. Nothing Eva couldn't fix. "You shouldn't have shot 'em. They gonna come for us all tonight wid them sheets and torches."

"They got your wife in there?" asked Esau, jerking his head at the cabin. Tom nodded, and Esau went to rip the barricade off the door.

Nelson looked down at Tom with that quiet, calculating way he had. He leaned on the stock of his rifle.

"You wanted us to just let 'em kill you?" said Nelson.

"Naw. But for God's sake," said Tom, rolling slowly to all fours, "Where the hell you learn to shoot like that, Nelson?"

"Dunno," grunted Nelson. "You can walk?"

"Yeah. Damn it, I can walk." Nelson helped the bigger man to his feet.

"I'll take you to Eva," said the Indian. But Tom shook his head. "I'm gonna get my affairs together first. The bastards got my papers. I'm sure that high-steppin' cracker bastard just gonna forge my signature anyhow. He just wanted to see me scairt."

"Is you scared?" asked Nelson. His flat black eyes were crinkled at the edges. Sometimes it was hard to tell if he was amused or serious. He always seemed to be a bit of both.

Tom barked a laugh. "Sure as the Devil is workin', Nelson. Sure I'm scared. But I think your scream scared me more than these bastards did."

As soon as Esau LaLaurie got the door open, Tom's wife and daughter came rushing out. They smothered him with kisses and wails, to which he gave a loud protest.

"What the hell y'all fussin' about? You let me stay out here n' get the black beat off me, when I showed you more than once how to use that gun in the corner there..."

Nelson pretended not to see the tears that streamed down Tom Shanter's cheeks.

♞

A few nights later Eva found the note slipped under the pot of rosemary on her step. Someone must have put it there while she was tending to another family down in the Low Rivers section of Rue Cher.

It had been a quiet past few days. Almost too quiet.

The note said: I need to see you. Sundown, at the bridge. -Renard

She crumpled it immediately and tossed it in her flowerbed. But as the day wore on she fetched it out. Smoothed it out on the table, tracing the fancy lettering of his signature with a fingertip. She imagined Renard sitting down to write it, getting frustrated, embarassed, and recklessly bold in turns.

She imagined lots of things. His lips coming down over hers. The heat of his body, sudden and fierce, pressed against her breasts. The urgent way he had gripped at her dress, as if he wanted nothing more than to tear it down the seams and mount her right there on the porch, among the smell of dahlias and honeysuckle. His mouth...

Her thighs trembled at the memory. A sweet memory with a bitter aftertaste.

They could not be together. Not here, in Louisiana. Likely not ever.

He was playing her for a fool. Everyone knew Gaspard Mauricette, Renard's father, had come down to Rue Cher to do his whoring. Who was to say Renard was any different- just 'cause he talked nicer than most white men and hung around colored folks and brought Eva books and flowerpots and sat on her porch and smoked sweet tobacco cigarettes and ate off her cracked plates with no complaints. Renard had a wife.

A horrible bitch of a wife, thought Eva, slamming her coffeepot down on the table.

Her gaze fell about the cabin that had been her grandmother's, and her mother's. Three generations of healers had worked under this roof. Theirs was an old and important practice- for who could Rue Cher turn to, if she couldn't be their healer?

Eva needed children- a daughter- to carry on her legacy. She had to do right by these people who had always done right by her. The proper thing to do would be to stop chasing after some white man she could never have and settle down with one of her own.

Better she forget about Renard. Better she stop thinking about him and tell him not to bring himself around here anymore. He was rich, wasn't he? He could afford all kinds of doctors and medicines. He didn't need her and it was better they stopped pretending that he did.

A fish and a bird may fall in love, but where they gonna build the nest?   So the old saying went.

Her mind made up, she did not go to the bridge and see Renard. Instead, she cleaned her teeth and took herself to bed.

CHAPTER FOUR

One way or another Amelie Mordant arrived at the Mauricette house, despite Renard's previous protests. Renard found her waiting there for him one afternoon and was justly furious. His mother and sister's plaintive entreaties went unheard, and she was forbidden from returning. His curses were vulgar enough to raise the dead, and for days the household went on silently and meekly in his presence.

But not a week passed before Renard took to bed with a sudden and violent illness. He lay there in a blind haze of pain, vaulting in and out of sleep. And the Madame Mauricette saw no one better fit than the darling Amelie, who showed up at the right time, insisted on tending to him herself, and refused to hear of sending for a doctor.

Renard's illness took a curious form. He spent most of it unconscious. Sometimes he saw shadows on the wall, terrifying shadows, that danced and laughed in macabre delight. Sometimes he saw a tall dark-haired woman bending over him. The visions were so real he could even feel the tips of her braid brush his cheek.

Snatches of quick conversation came to him through the haze:

...no signs of recovery...

So inconvenient, he never thinks of us at all...

...Glad you are with him, dear, he needs his wife...

Oh no, Madame. I have it under control. No one must enter this room but me. It is all perfectly alright.

Once he managed to sit up. Strangely, the pain was not in his leg, but his brain. He saw three of everything he looked at.

A tall woman with very dark hair loomed in front of him. She patted his leg gently. Her other hand held a steaming cup.

The room itself was hazy with some kind of smoke. He perceived a small brazier burning in the fireplace. A woman's form emerged from the smoke; she had something over her nose and mouth, but the green eyes glowed like gems.

"Who are you?" he asked, not believing what he saw.

"Your wife." Her eyes smiled.

"I have no wife," he said. "I am divorced."

He nodded off again. Amelie Mordant left Renard sleeping, removed her mask, and let herself out of the room. She turned to the curious faces of his mother and sister. They were dressed for a party, and looked anxious to leave. Some smoke escaped the room; Fiona Mauricette coughed into her fist.

"What is that smell?" she whined.

"A draught I am mixing. He will survive the night," said Amelie, privately amused by their vain attempts to look concerned. It was no secret to her that the pair of them despised Renard.

"Oh, wonderful. We are just concerned, dear, about leaving you here alone..." Madame cast a suspicious eye at the servants.

"No trouble," Amelie oozed. "I would not leave my darling's side."

"It seems so strange that your father allowed you to learn doctoring. I never heard of anything in all my years. In my days, women were content to be just wives. How times change," tittered Renard's mother.

"You flatter me," was Amelie's mechanical response.

Madame pinched Amelie's cheek. The young Mordant frowned, but let the impertinence slide.

"We will be back by midafternoon tomorrow," said the older woman, squeezing her hands into a pair of soft gloves. "You are sure he will be alright?"

"Certainly."

Renard's mother hesitated for a moment, and her smile faltered. Even she did not fully trust the beautiful, smooth-talking young woman. There was something predatory about her that Madame's small brain struggled to comprehend. But in the end selfishness won out. She left with Fiona for the party.

Amelie watched them leave through the study window. Then she promptly ordered the negro servants away. She had no authority to do so, of course, but they made haste to obey her anyway. They were terrified of her.

She shut the study door and began her mission. Amelie spared no thought for the child she had left behind at her father's house, nor the sleeping man in the adjacent room. Only one thing occupied her thoughts, and she had a day and a half left to find it.

What Amelie searched for in particular was a book, which her father had alleged was located in Gaspard Mauricette's old study. The book itself would have raised hairs among the gentlefolk of Louisiana, even if it had not contained a particular piece of evidence that must at all costs be kept from the wrong hands. The journal contained some of her mother's Conjuring secrets, and an account of Amelie's birth.

Renard was key to locating the whereabouts of such a book, for without Renard she would not have gotten ten feet past the anxious Madame Mauricette or her tattletale servants. Masquerading as a concerned wife was easy for Amelie. So she had devised this scheme with the help of a little poison and a lot of masquerade. But all these last few days had achieved her was a growing frustration and no results. And the suspicion of the dim-witted Mauricettes.

Gaspard Mauricette and Louis Mordant had been lifelong friends. Sharing women, horses, finances, secrets. Even, if the rumors were true, a bed. Amelie and Renard had been pawns in their scheme to unite the two families once and for all, bringing the fortunes together under law. Gaspard would control Renard, and Louis would control Amelie. Together they could work on wresting their land back from the reprehensible negroes, righting the mistakes of their soft-headed forefathers, and forging an empire Louisiana would never forget, in one fell swoop.

In the beginning Amelie wondered why she and Renard's marriage had been a necessity in this arrangement. So typical of her father to insist on grand symbolic gestures that ultimately meant nothing. In any event, she had developed an obsession with her handsome, arrogant Mauricette husband. An obsession with destroying him.

Their antagonism towards each other, which had only developed once he got a true sense of her personality, had almost ruined their fathers' plans, so off Renard went to war at Gaspard's insistence.

Then Gaspard foolishly got a heart attack and died.

Amelie was still searching the study when she heard the door to Renard's room bang open and shut. She flew out into the hallway to check on him. He was still in the smoky room, dead asleep. An innocent-looking negro girl was polishing the floor down the hallway.

"Did you go inside the room?" barked Amelie, shutting the door. "I ordered you all downstairs!"

"No Miss!" chattered the girl, trembling in fright. But there seemed something deliberately false about her affections of distress, which irritated Amelie all the more. She scowled and bore down on her.

"I swear I didn't! I just been here- sweeping- doin'

my job-"

"Mister Mauricette must not be disturbed!" Amelie delivered the wench a vicious backhand and sent her scurrying down the stairs.

She returned to the study, turning out all the drawers in search of a false bottom, a switch...anything. Not two minutes had passed before someone came banging on the door again.

"Miss Mordant! Miss Mordant!" a servant hollered. "You best come quick!"

Storming with rage, Amelie burst out the room. "What the devil is the matter with you niggers?"

"Your dog found his way in the cellar and we can't get 'im out," said the servant quickly. He wrung his hands in exaggerated consternation. "He likely to bite us and we all scared. And we afraid 'cause Master Gaspard used to say there was a alligator livin' down there and we afraid the gator's gonna get your dog-"

the rest devolved into nonsensical creole babble.

"Be silent!" hissed Amelie. "Show me the way."

Amelie's dog, a fluffy white pooch, was a vicious and temperamental beast. She fancied the dog more than she did her child; indeed a dog was a sight more useful than a child. Of course the negroes would fear him, the simple creatures. She followed the servant's lead, not sure whether to be amused or furious. Amelie highly doubted there was actually an alligator in the Mauricette cellar. But perhaps, she realized cunningly, Gaspard had told the servants there was...to keep them away from something.

Surely her clever little Bisou had not led her straight to the book?

The cellar door was located in the kitchens, which were a few feet from the house. As she swept through the door the cook and the scullery boy eyed her fearfully. The cook was a shriveled old woman about as tall as a gentleman's walking stick. The boy was shrunken and underfed. The man who had summoned Amelie opened the cellar door with effort. The door was extremely heavy and barred with twisted metal. The hinges squealed loosely; the man had to hold it open for her. She discerned, from the cellar depths, Bisou's agitated barking.

"Why was this door left open?" she demanded.

"The child wanted to see the gator," squeaked the cook. She clutched the boy's shoulders.

"I will have him punished," Amelie declared. It did not occur to her that a small child could not have possibly held open such a heavy door for long.

"All of you will be punished, in fact. Find me a light."

The cook lit her a lamp and gave the other servant a funny look.

Probably thinking: why did Miss Amelie not simply call the dog to her?

"Keep this door open," she ordered. And she descended the steps, clutching her skirts and holding the light aloft. The cellar had a dampness about it. It smelled like a swamp. She wondered why on earth such a hellpit had been built into the house. Likely to throw troublesome negroes into. Which struck Amelie as an amusing idea. She might lock the little boy down there, for letting Bisou escape.

She reached the landing and immediately stepped in a puddle of something foul. Cursing, she held up the light high. It bounced off slimy walls and the huddled, snarling form of her dog. "Bisou," she crooned. "What have you gotten into, you troublesome thing?"

Whatever the dog's response, she didn't hear it. The cellar door banged shut and the square of light above the staircase vanished. Amelie was trapped.

The Mauricette Butler hurried into the master

bedroom, Eva LaLaurie not far behind him. Thin clouds of smoke billowed out the door when they opened it.

"Thunderation!" gasped Eva. She hurried to the little brazier and snatched it off the fire with a poker. Her eyes streaming, she flung it out the window that Betty the maid had opened.

"Poison," she declared grimly. She fanned the stinking smoke away from her face and turned to the bed. Renard was beginning to sit up with great effort. His curly hair clouded around his face, trailing messily over glazed eyes. His fists clenched in the sheets. He looked extremely sick.

This was the first she had seen of Renard since their encounter a week ago. He looked like an entirely different person.

"Can you hear me, Mister Renard?" said Eva, pressing a hand to his forehead.

"Work fast," said John. "You ain't got much time."

"I...can...hear you," mumbled Renard. His eyes peeled open again. They were red-rimmed and rheumy.

"A minute ago he looked dead," said John. "I told him we sent for you and he tried to sit up."

Betty and Eva helped the big man out into the hallway, where the air was clean. He took long, dry, shuddering coughs.

Eva took something out of the little pouch at her waist and waved it under his nose. Renard shook his head like a dog, stumbled back, and vomited in the doorframe. Betty gave a strangled exclamation- she hated cleaning up Sick.

"Eva?" he muttered, looking up into the healer woman's face. His eyes looked like a madman's.

"Yes, it's me," said Eva. She turned to John. "How long he been like this?"

"A week," said John. "Had a fight with that woman an' took sick right after. We found she was poisonin' him when Betty went in to get somethin' and got a whiff of that smoke. I recognized the smell immediately."

"Mercy," said Eva. "Y'all must be loyal to him."

"Well," said John, a touch defensively, "I wouldn't jump in front of a train for him. I respect the man, that's all. And I know his folks don't have a brain to share between them. He pays us well."

Not exactly a glowing praise, but well enough. Eva put a shoulder under Renard's arm. "Come on, Renard, let's get you downstairs."

"I can walk," he muttered.

"Naw, you can't," snapped Eva. "We ain't goin' far."

"My coat," he said. "I want to leave."

Eva glanced at John. He shook his head. "Not yet. He's got to be there when they let his wife out the cellar, or she'll rain hell on all the servants. He's got to tell her it was all his idea. Tell her he made them do it."

Even in his disoriented state Renard did not miss the general drift of John's words. "Do what? Lie to Amelie?" he mumbled.

"They locked your wife in the cellar to get you out."

Renard blinked. "Oh."

"You got to cover for them," said Eva insistently. "Will you do it?"

His brow worked. For a moment she feared he would not understand. "Yes," he said. "Yes, for the love of God. Get her out of there."

So Eva sat him up in a chair, and brought him his

169

trousers, boots and cane. She helped him into his clothes. There was no time for embarrassment. The maids fluttered about, trying to find work that would make them invisible for the next hour. Nervous wrecks, all. The scheme had been John's idea, but they could all suffer punishment.

Once Renard was dressed he put his head in his hands. He had a pounding, horrible headache. The inside of his mouth felt mossy and disgusting.

"Bring her in," she said. John left the room. In a few minutes they could hear Amelie raging out of the kitchens. Eva prepared to make herself scarce, but Renard grabbed her hand.

"I'm coming," he told her. His eyes found hers and narrowed. "To see you. Tonight."

She looked around. "No," she said. "This is all too much for me, Renard. I can't be hangin' around you. You got a wife, and she's crazy as all hell."

"Eva. Please."

Amelie's enraged vituperations grew louder. Eva cast her eyes to the ceiling.

"Eva," he said again. It was not a question.

"Fine," she whispered. "Don't be seen."

He kissed her hand, and she was gone.

Renard took a deep breath as Eva hurried out the front door. He still felt like throwing up in his lap. His vision spun when he looked at something for too long. But stronger than the pain was the anger, an anger that reared inside him like a furious red dragon.

When Amelie Mordant exploded through the doorway, he was alone. The servants had disappeared with Eva.

News of what had happened spread through Rue Cher faster than a dog with its tail on fire. Eva shut the cabin door and didn't answer it for anyone, not even Sam, who came 'round to confirm the story.

She spent the rest of the day in bed. She couldn't explain the feeling twisting up her guts, no more than she could explain the sudden urge to sob uncontrollably into her mattress.

When Eva had received word from John about what was happening at the Mauricette house, she had not believed him. She wondered if the servants at the house would be punished, and she was scared for them. She was scared for the people of Rue Cher too, after what had happened with Tom Shanter. And she was scared for herself.

With everything going on it was foolish to even think about Renard Mauricette. Yet if she had not gone with John, no doubt the smoking herbs that madwoman had planted would have made him very sick or even killed him.

I'm coming to see you. Tonight.

Renard might have been a fool...but Eva was more the fool. She should have refused him. A married man!

She eventually got out of bed and went to draw herself a bath. The water was freezing and unpleasant. She found herself reaching for one of her rare soaps, a gift from a woman across the river whose daughter she had cured of measles. Next she let her hair out of its pins and washed it thoroughly. She scrubbed herself head to toe and put on a clean dress.

Yet it was not until many hours later, when the moon was burning overhead, that she heard the scraping knock on the door. She jumped out of her skin. The room seemed to shrink around her.

For a moment she considered staying quiet and letting him think she wasn't home, like she had almost done the first time he'd kissed her...

But she walked to the door and opened it.

Renard had certainly looked better. His hair was rumpled, three long scratches were raked across his cheek, and he had a week's worth of stubble dusted over his chin. But he gave a wide grin when she opened the door, and stepped through and swept her in his arms. He smelled clean and fresh as he always did.

She squeaked and tried to push away, but he hugged her tighter and swung her in a quick circle.

"Renard!" she laughed. He kicked the door shut and turned to her again. The smile was gone; he looked serious, but happy.

"Eva. Eva, Eva, I'm so sorry."

She smoothed her skirts. Nerves were turning her legs and hands to jelly. In the low kerosene light he looked nearly irresistible. And he smelled divine- certainly better than he had when she'd lifted him off the bed that morning.

But no! She couldn't think of that! She was furious with him! She stepped back and tossed her head.

"So why you didn't tell me you was married, Renard?"

He jerked back. "Pardon?"

She stepped away from his embrace. "Your wife. She came and gave me a visit. Even before you got sick."

"Amelie?"

"Yes," said Eva. "The very same. So now you remember you married? But when we were kissin' and carryin' on in here-"

"Yes, I'm married. But we're separated."

This would have made sense to Eva if he had been

someone from Rue Cher. Folks got married and separated all the time; sometimes they wound their way back to each other and sometimes they didn't. But she had reasons to be suspicious of Renard Mauricette and his mysterious, insane, surprise-wife, for the simple fact that he was white and rich and had no business messing with a girl like her anyhow.

Even though she had, maybe, wanted him to mess with her.

"Really," she scoffed.

"Are you listening to me? We were separated. And now divorced. We were married legally but definitely not under God. Or any church I know of. And I'm not in love with her. Heaven forbid I call that bitch my wife."

"So I'm supposed to believe that?"

"Yes," said Renard, as if she was simple. "I don't lie."

"That's what all men say!"

"I can't speak for all men."

Why did he have to look at her like that? And now he was handing her the papers. Should she bother reading them? She did bother. It was true- the date on the paper was a couple of weeks past. Eva had never heard of anyone getting a divorce. It just wasn't done.

"Come with me," he demanded.

"Excuse me? I'm not leavin' this house tonight. No, sir."

"Don't be difficult, Eva."

"I got every right to be mad."

"I explained myself. I had no idea that woman would show her face around me again."

"But you still shoulda told me you had a wife-"

"Why? What does it matter? I know how I feel about you. What else is important?"

"Oh? And how do you feel 'bout me?"

"Right now? Like turning you over my knee," he growled.

"Just try it!"

They were getting nowhere. Renard rubbed his face. When he spoke again it was in a different tone of voice.

"Come with me. I have dinner waiting. Let me apologize, Eva, damn you."

Against her better judgment, she returned him the papers. He tucked them into his breast pocket. Then Renard took her hand and led her outside. He was limping heavily, but he had a strawberry roan saddled and tied to her fencepost. His leg must be a bit better, then... She had never seen him ride a horse to meet her before.

They said no more words to each other. Eva was angry and confused and proud. Renard- well, Renard was his usual enigmatic self. He lifted her onto the back of the horse and swung himself up behind her on the opposite side.

Eva's heart beat solidly in her chest. His arms came up around her and held the reins. She leaned back and the sweet heat of him enveloped her. He smelled like soap and leather.

What if they were seen? They wouldn't be seen. Did she care? No. She didn't. Did he? Of course not. Renard was still a Mauricette, and the local folks knew his name, if not his face. If he wanted Eva to sit up on a horse with him, he damn well would have her up there.

"Where we goin'?" she murmured. He had mentioned dinner...

"You'll see," he said.

And she trusted him, even as they trotted away from Rue Cher, up towards the Mauricette house. She thought he might veer off and take her into the woods. Where no prying eyes could see, where they could liason in utter peace and secrecy. To her surprise- and horror- they instead headed straight up the hill towards the Mauricette mansion.

CHAPTER FIVE

"Renard!" she gasped. "Up there?"

She twisted to see his face, but he gripped her tighter. "You don't have anything to worry about," he said to her. "You're with me."

"If someone sees us-"

"I dismissed the servants after you left," he said. "They had enough to deal with. And Amelie is gone. It's just the two of us."

"Do I trust you?" Eva moaned, wringing her hands.

He wrapped his arm strongly about her waist and squeezed her so tight she yelped. A feather-like touch; his lips and teeth at the soft skin of her throat. The touch sent cool tingles up the ridge of her spine. "You must."

By the time they arrived at the big house Eva was nearly shaking with anxiety. He had not dismissed all the servants. His right-hand man John was there; he tipped his hat sarcastically to Eva, and led the horse away.

Renard led her through the house. Candles and braziers were lit along the staircase. Eva could only stare at the extravagant splendor. Earlier she had come with a mission to save Renard, and had hardly examined the house. Now she could take it all in, with all its finery and opulence.

Of course she knew that black folks had built this house, every brick and board. And it had been their labor- the labor of her grandmothers, great-grandmothers, grandfathers, and so on, that had furnished it, staffed it, and fed the people who lived there. She was not bitter about this. But it did make her uncomfortable. She looked at Renard, who seemed so used to the richness of his surroundings that he scarcely paid it attention. He led her down a long hallway where the portraits of his ancestors glared at her. She defiled their house with every step.

Renard was a product of this environment of grotesque excess, surely as she was. Only their positions were diametrically opposed. Eva had been born into poverty and she would likely die there. Renard Mauricette could never understand poverty, just as you couldn't explain to a fish how a bird took to its wings and flew. So could he ever understand her?

They came to the high-ceiling dining room. Candles were lit; someone had laid out a modest feast. There was a small roast chicken, served with a wine sauce, sweet potatoes and dandelion greens. Renard pulled out the chair for her. She sat.

Moving as if through a dream, they dug into the food. Renard said nothing so neither did she. Eva found her appetite unmarred. And when they were finished eating, he cleared their plates himself and brought them to the kitchens outside. Then, returning, he led her up the stairs.

They went up two flights. In a different wing of the house, designed by a romantic perhaps, a door opened out into a small balcony. They ducked through.

"Watch your step," said Renard, helping her down. He did not remove his arm from her waist.

A small couch had been moved out here. And Eva found herself under a latticework of stars.

They were high up, on top of the world. A breeze blew sweetly against her face, and the crickets were singing in a language as old as the forest. She observed the faint lights of Rue Cher winking out now that night was come, and with the moon's assistance she saw past the sloping hills, where the earth disappeared on a soft curve and went on for untold miles. Even the sweet stink of the swamp, which came on the high notes of the wind, was pleasant to her now. Renard moved so he was behind her with his arms around her waist. The top of her head tucked beneath his chin.

"I want to know," he said quietly, "What you are thinking."

"Why you brought me here," she replied.

"Isn't it obvious?"

"Maybe," she said. She took a deep breath. "Renard-you know we can't do this."

"Tell me why," he said. She turned to face him.

"You want me to put it plain? 'Cause I'm black, and 'cause you white. I'm a poor girl from the village and

185

you got-" she flung her arms out, "all of this. How long you want to keep this up with me? A week? A month? Before you go runnin' back to your fancy wife? Before your fancy wife decides to kill me?"

"As long as we can," he told her. "And no one is going to hurt you on my account, Eva."

"I got a future to plan," she pressed on. "And I can't see how you fit in it, with your family and your big money. Amelie told me herself-"

"Told you what?" he said sharply.

"She said she was gonna burn me and my house down if I kept foolin' with you. What you think is gonna happen if we start seein' each other more? Livin' together?" She regretted adding that last part. It sounded presumptuous.

"Nobody is going to hurt you," said Renard firmly. "Understand?"

"How you know that?"

"Eva," said Renard. He shook his head. Taking her hand, he led her to the very edge of the balcony. "You see all that?"

"Yes." She saw the little lights of Rue Cher, and the swamp, and the bridge.

"No, look where I'm pointin'. What do you see?"

She looked. "The horizon," she said.

"Exactly. You and me can go anywhere. We're not bound down to this place. I have money, I have title and lands. But there is no law that says I have to stay here. And no law that says you have to, either."

Was he asking her to run away with him? Eva gulped. "You want me to go somewhere with you?" she said in a small voice.

"If you want to," he began, but then he shook his

head. "No. I mean yes, yes I am. If not now, then in the future. If not tomorrow, then next year."

Her head spun. "Renard, we ain't even known each other two months. I can't leave Rue Cher. That's my people down there."

"I can wait," he said. His eyes burned like two coins. A flush had crept up his face, and he squeezed her hand hard. Eva knew he meant every word he had said. That was the way with Renard- he said no less than what was in his heart.

He kept talking, his words spilling over each other. It was uncharacteristic of him. "You are an honest woman. You're a good woman. I see it in you, the way you work with your people. Nothing makes me feel so good as your presence- and I'd rather be shot all over again than see you unhappy or miserable."

"I'm not unhappy," said Eva, though two tears had flashed into her eyes.

"I know," he said. He gripped her hands so tightly she swore the bones crunched. "I swear, we can keep seein' each other like this as long as you want. And when you're ready, I'll be here. I don't look at no other woman but you, Evie, white or black. And that's the heart's truth I'm telling you."

In his passion his accent had slipped towards the country drawl of his youth.

"What if somethin' happens?" she said quietly. "What if they catch us-"

" Who is 'they?' Well, I'm tellin' you that 'they' won't. And even then I'd risk it all," declared Renard. "Life is too short to be scared of it. Give it a chance."

Maybe Renard Mauricette's roof wasn't nailed on all that tight. Or maybe he was dipping all his words in honey to hide some rotten intention.

But Eva LaLaurie found herself compelled to believe every word he'd said.

In truth she had made her decision already about Renard. She had fallen for him. What a wonderful mess. She stepped into the circle of his arms but he held her out by the shoulder.

"Wait a minute," he told her, fumbling with something in his pocket.

To Eva's eternal surprise he produced a tiny gold ring with a large pear-cut opal settled in a nest of miniature diamonds. Of course, Eva didn't know all that, until he told her later. She couldn't have told you the difference between an opal and a ruby if you put a gun to her head. Still, you had to be stone blind to not see that this ring was quality- and it was old. Her mouth hit the wood-stained floor.

"This is for you."

"You must be plumb crazy," she said.

"Give me your hand," said Renard.

"Renard- I can't. Absolutely not. You must want to see me jailed. I walk around with a thing like that, folks will say I stole it."

"Your hand," said Renard, as if he hadn't heard her. He raised it for himself and slid the ring on her left index finger. It fit perfectly. He smiled and pulled her close.

"A soldier I fought with bought this ring," said Renard, holding her shoulders and pulling away again. He spoke fast so she wouldn't cut him off. "A black man named Henry Bede. Bought it in Paris for his girl back in Tucson. Spent nearly half his savings; we almost shipped out before the jeweler had it finished. He was buzzing like a bee about the Commander beggin' him to wait. Finally it arrived."

"But-"

Renard held up her hand to the moonlight, turning it

this way and that. Eva had beautiful hands. Strong, sturdy hands.

"It didn't matter cause old Harry got a dear john as soon as we reached the trenches. The girl had taken up with someone else. Nearly broke Harry to pieces. And he said he couldn't look at the damn thing anymore, so he gave it to me. Said maybe I might be more lucky in love. He was a philosophical kind of bastard."

"He didn't take the ring back?"

"Harry died," said Renard simply, "in the same blast that almost took my leg. He got the full blow of it. And I kept his ring ever since."

She looked again at the storied ring, and her heart gave a little squeeze. Of course she would keep it. She kept all her gifts. But...

"Renard, you know I can't wear this around anyway. It's too fine for someone like me." But its beauty had snared her, and Eva was no longer trying to convince Renard, but herself.

"Someone like who? You know, I always thought in the right clothes you'd be finer than all these other ladies. It's something about you."

"Soul," she said, still looking at the ring. She smiled.

"Yes. That."

He raised her hands to his lips. His kiss brushed her knuckles, fingertips, the inside of her wrist...

"Please," she whispered. She didn't know what she was asking for.

"I don't care," he murmured. "Wear it if you like. And know, Eva, I would buy you a hundred rings like this and more, if only to remind you of what's in my heart. I will prove my feelings to you in any way you desire." His yellowish cat's eyes burned into hers.

And, as if hypnotized, Eva found herself stepping towards him into his arms. Her head tilted back. The sharp angles of his features blurred, and then the imprint of his lips wiped out any last traces of protest. She tasted him. She felt him, lean and muscled, his body hot, hot, hotter than hell.

He leaned back against the wooden railing and brought the length of her against him. Eva's skin seemed to merge with the blue darkness of the night. He might have been kissing a handful of starlight. Renard felt the whole of her curvy body, full-figured, lush, overflowing. And then he deepened the kiss, and then they were sinking into each other, his hands roving where he knew they shouldn't...but who was to stop him? No one; certainly not Eva.

He ruched up the fabrics of her skirts and petticoats with one fist, and then clenching her torso tightly to his own, his lips poised to catch her whimpers, his other hand crept upwards to the fork of her legs.

Eva's breath caught as he found the source of her

wetness. He turned and braced her against the railing. The polished wood dug into her spine, she gripped the muscles of his arms. His eyes found hers.

"You're a virgin?"

She nodded. His fingers continued to ply her slickness and he looked at her as if expecting a response. But no. She did not want him to stop. Her eyes drifted closed. It felt good, good, gooood...

"Are you afraid?" he murmured, his teeth closing around the soft flesh of her earlobe.

"No," she said.

"Then come here."

Practically lifting her into his arms, Renard carried her back into the house. The heady romance of the night sky vanished. Here, in this old house, Eva felt again like she was dreaming. She seemed to be watching it all unfold from a distance, that rational and sensible part of her head screaming at her to stop before it was too late (too late for what?). But the more powerful part, the sensing part, was far louder. Her heart beat in time with Renard's. She knew he would do nothing to hurt her.

He stopped and propped her against the wall. She kissed him urgently, passionately, messily. He groaned into her mouth and found the buttons on her dress. He took two handfuls of fabric and pulled. Hard. Buttons chattered to the floor but neither paid them mind; Renard had yanked the bodice down her shoulders and found her breasts.

"What's this?" he murmured, lifting the little bag of Sam's protection still hanging around her neck. Eva laughed, embarassed. "Oh, somethin' Sam gave me..."

"Mmm." He turned his attention back to her lips and his hands skimmed up to cup the recently-bared flesh.

Eva's breasts were full and round and heavy. He weighed them in both hands but did not bring his mouth to them; not yet. Every inch of her was his now, and he had thought about this for untold weeks, and now that Eva was his to savor, he would take his time.

He turned her around so her breasts flattened against the wall. Eva felt his mouth at her throat and thought she might die of anticipation. His hands ruched up her dress, as if wanting to tear the rest off and leave her stark naked before him. Indeed she would not have minded if he took her right there on the polished floor. But instead he gripped the ample flesh of her buttocks, hard, hard enough that she whimpered. He roved around her hips and found her pocketbook again, and to Eva's surprise his fingers touched on something that made her gasp and jump back against him.

Renard held her there, twitching, panting, and he held her there as her whimpers turned to stifled, surprised screams. Only when she strained and sighed in blissful relief did he release her, and then they moved on again, Eva clutching the ruined fabric of her dress to her breasts. He led her to a bedroom- the master bedroom.

They fell upon the bed, stripped that morning and prepared with clean-smelling sheets. Renard straddled her, imprisoning her between both his thighs. The deep scar of the old wound seemed unimportant; indeed he hardly felt it. At once his fingers had slid inside her again. When he spoke it was in perfect creole. She understood every word.

"I would make love to you in every room of this house, on every piece of furniture, in every doorway," he said. "I would make you scream my name to these rafters, day and night, until you forgot all other words."

"Do it, then," she responded in her own language.

He laughed and drew the rest of her dress off. Eva's hands set to work on his clothes. She traced the scars that had laid out across his torso like a spider's web, the scars on his face. He hovered over her on his elbows and let her explore him. Eva was no stranger to men's bodies, but the darkness of the bedroom, and anticipation of the forbidden act they were about to perform, lent a new kind of mystery to what she touched.

Renard was lean, but muscled well and hardened to a finish. She wished the room were not so dark...

He angled himself over her. The blunt edge of his penis, the one thing she had been too shy to touch, skimmed along her thigh. Hot and heavy. A pistol. His lips hovered a moment from her own as he lined himself up with her entrance.

"Tell me now," he said. "Tell me now, or I don't know if I'll be able to stop."

Would he pull away? Even if she had wanted to say no?

"Yes," said Eva. And taking that for assent, Renard wrapped his left hand loosely around her throat. He plunged his cock inside her.

Eva's eyes flew open; she nearly screamed. He covered her face with kisses. "I'm so sorry, I'm so sorry, love. It won't hurt again."

"Go on," she said, knowing that it would. He was not a small man, and Eva was still virgin-tight...Renard would have to take his time.

And take his time he did. At first. Renard's hips moved in slow, deliberate rhythm. He treated her like a delicate, delicate thing. He held her under the full weight of his body, imprisoning her, so even when she was slick and moist and ready to feel more, to go faster, she had to wait.

There was no hurrying in love, and they had all night. His cock seemed to reach her heart. The sensation of being filled to the limit fired off explosions of ecstasy within her; and that it was Renard Mauricette, her friend, her lover, buried to the hilt inside her, nearly overwhelmed Eva. He saw she was ready and his hips drove in faster. The hand around her throat tightened once, then released, then tightened again.

"Tell me," he murmured in between thrusts. He burned against her like a live coal. "Tell me when you feel it coming."

It was the same thing he had done to her outside the room, against the wall. As if tugging on some invisible switch. Only this time it came on her like a wave, a hurricane, a fearsome, wonderful thing. Her whimpers turned to screams. Her screams shaped around the vowels of his name, and she was shouting it to the bedroom, to the house, to the world. His teeth closed around her throat again, and he was at once plunging into her most sensitive, pleasureable parts and teasing her nerves, making her submit to his consuming will, and the passion that drove him harder, deeper into her.

"Eva," he grunted. "How do you do this to me..."

Renard, Renard...

And when the climax hit it moved through them at the same time. They might have been one body and one soul, immolated on a pyre of a love they could not find a name for. He burst inside her. And for a moment Eva felt like the whole world had stopped.

♞

She woke in the early hours, when the sun was drawing up over the sky. Funny, the sun, that never cared about the futilities of men. The rules they invented for themselves. Why couldn't she stay here, her thighs sticky with Renard's seed, struggling to breathe under the heavily muscled arm he had thrown across her chest?

Such was the unfairness of things. Eva breathed very deeply, savoring the moment. She turned to the man beside her. In sleep the lines of Renard's face seemed all the more pronounced. His sharp, wolfish features looked almost puppyish. The too-long lashes brushed his high cheekbones.

What was it about him?

In many ways he still felt as foreign to her as he had the first night they had met. Yet the sinister, heavy aura she had perceived about him seemed a thing of the past. Had it vanished, once she had saved him from Amelie Mordant? She must ask Sam.

The thought of Sam now sent reality crashing over Eva with horrible immediacy. Her eyes darted about the room. She was in the Mauricette house. The richest people in Rue Cher. The opal ring sitting heavily on her left hand seemed to tighten. And now the finery of the oak paneling, the high mirror framed with gilded bronze, the heady scent of lavender potpourri, the elaborately painted ceiling detailing a scene of roses, clouds, cherubs and angels danced mockingly before her. White angels. White cherubs.

The weight of what had happened crushed her. Gone was the passion of the night before where these things, though no less real, had seemed so much more insignificant. This was another world she had been seduced into. And it was not her world- it could never be. In fact, it was dangerous to even pretend.

She had to get up. She had to get out.

She started towards her dress, but remembered, with growing horror, Renard had ripped the bodice to pieces.

Eva pressed a fist to her mouth. She stifled the urge to scream. What could she do? Flee the house, take the forest path to Rue Cher...but even then, what if the men saw her?

As if sensing her distress, Renard stirred. His eyes fluttered and he realized she was not in bed with him. He raised himself, his sleepy eyes scanning the room- and found her. At once he was awake.

"Eva- What's the matter?"

Oh, of course she was crying. Hot, stormy, silent tears. She opened her mouth and choked on the response. The hand clutching the dress trembled.

Renard slid off the bed and pulled her to him roughly. His arms wrapped around her and he drew her streaming face to his shoulder.

"Don't cry," he said. "I have you. Please don't cry."

"I got to go," she said. "I got to leave."

"You don't," he said. "You can stay. I want you to stay."

His lips found hers. Gentle but firm, his hands held her arms at her sides. She let him kiss her, make love-words to her, draw her again to the deep bed. He slid her under him and was inside her again with a smooth thrust.

Eva's arms wrapped around his neck and his body crushed her breasts between them. Somehow he must have sensed that she did not want him to be gentle. He fucked her. Again, again, and then faster, then rougher. Eva's nails dug into the muscles of his arms. He battered at her with growing force, as if he wanted to fuck her off the bed. The frame rocked obscenely. Were they making love- were they fighting?

Her orgasm came hard, and she shook like a leaf and so did he. Eva felt the hot ropes of semen leaking out of her once he pulled away. You got to do somethin' about that, she thought, or there'll be a baby.

Perhaps Renard was thinking the same thing. He fell against her and his hands laced with hers and drew them up over her head.

"If you get pregnant, Eva-"

"I won't."

"But if you do. I will stand by you."

"You won't be makin' any pretenses with me?" she

said timidly.

He sat up on his elbows suddenly. Renard could never make promises without the full intensity of his personality showing through. He moved over her and made her look into his eyes. They were dark with desire. And yes, honesty. Renard never lied.

"Pretenses? Never I," he said. "Never with you."

And to Eva's own astonishment, she believed him.

CHAPTER SIX

Over the next month Eva found her life taking a strange new direction.

For one thing, she and Renard could no longer be seen in each other's company. Not openly. The rumors flew thick and fast about their heads. Better they not flaunt it and so draw disaster on each other.

And in the beginning, the secrecy heightened the passion when they were together.

He came to see her at night. He had taken to walking the whole distance. And with all the exercise his limp had improved. She would hear a scratching at her door, her name murmured...and she would open it onto his grinning face. Then he would sweep her into his arms, kick the door shut...and well. Whatever went on after that was her business.

Sometimes they did not make love at all. Sometimes they went out into the very darkest night and walked through the forest and the swamp and talked. Sometimes Renard brought her books- all kinds of books on doctoring and medicine, even rare books, and sat quietly at her feet while she read them, her hands threading through his hair.

And what did she learn about him?

She learned that he was temperamental, passionate. She learned of his disdain for his own people, though he never put it in such plain terms. He hated the excess and waste of his class, their callousness, their cruelty, and their greed. Had he always felt that way? she asked him.

Always, he said, but never so much as when I came

home from France.

He did not need to tell her that what he had seen in those trenches had broken something inside him for good. When he returned home he could no longer pretend the rich planters, with all their money and airs, did not disgust him.

What did you see in the war? She would ask.

He always shook his head and changed the subject.

Eva was always afraid to ask the one question that tugged at her heart like a fishhook. Which was, if you hate your people so much, how come you don't just leave? She sensed she would not like the answer.

In her heart of hearts she entertained girlish dreams of running off with Renard, or building a cabin in the inner woods just for the two of them. But these were the dreams of country girls. The kind of dreams her mother and Nanny would have scoffed at, because they knew better.

Slowly dreams of that nature faded. She decided to live in the present. She started asking Renard about the nurses in the battlements. She drew from him long stories about their tools, and their procedures. She read and re-read Gray's Anatomy. And of course she still tended to the regular sore tooth, split finger or busted ankle, which popped up less frequently now that summer was coming to its end and folks were staying inside.

Eva began to dream of going to school.

It started with Renard casually mentioning a black female doctor he had heard of while in Boston. Her name was Louise Sadie Rumpler. She was from Alabama and she'd gone to New York medical college. Eva's eyes had nearly popped out of her head when Renard, at her insistence, scrounged up a newspaper clipping with Louise Rumpler's picture.

The thought became obsessive. She longed to know

211

more about this woman, but some shyness held her back from asking Renard. She did not want to seem like an eager country bumpkin. Once, casually, she asked Renard just how folks became doctors. He said they had to go through school twice, but he didn't know much about it. She gathered it was a rigorous- and expensive- field of study.

"You've got to know biology, chemistry, all of that," said Renard idly, turning the newspaper pages. "I was never good at these things. Equations? Maths? Pshaw. I preferred the arts."

Eva's heart sank. Chemistry? Biology? Eva's schooling, though accomplished through the best efforts of the Yankee woman who had arranged the Rue Cher schoolhouse, had been incomplete. And then some white folks across the river heard about the Yankee woman and promptly ran her out of town. So no, Eva didn't know the first thing about the sciences. Certainly not enough to have mattered. After that conversation she stopped asking Renard about medicine. It seemed a faraway, impossible dream. She might as well ask to be crowned Queen of Louisiana.

Right?

One afternoon they were outside taking air in the gardens. His family was not home. Another day spent alone, then, and Renard was showing her the plants that the servants tended to- exotic plants she had never seen. She wandered off on her own in the little maze. As she was lost in thought, Renard crept up behind her and brought his hand down playfully on the soft flesh of her backside. She jumped and squeaked.

"Don't think too much," he murmured. "I can tell you're thinking too much."

"Hmph!" said Eva. "And you don't think at all."

They heard noises suddenly. A high, fluting voice- Renard's mother.

"Oh damn," he said.

"I better leave," said Eva.

Instead he plucked a juicy hibiscus from the bush and tucked it behind her ear. "No. Come here."

He pulled her into an alcove in the garden.

Eva had at that point divested herself of her fears of being seen. She trusted Renard's good sense. He was daring, but never reckless.

They started to kiss. His lips pulled over hers, softly, tantalizingly. She tasted his tongue again, and his hands dug into the sensitive spot in her sides that made her squirm and giggle. It was as if Renard had learned the ways of love in France, along with the ways of war...Sometimes it truly felt like both were at play in his caresses.

His hands dropped lower. He cupped the soft, malleable flesh of her bottom. "You know, Eva," he murmured huskily, "I've never seen a woman with an ass like yours."

She hit him on the chest. "Renard," she hissed helplessly, still giggling. "If someone sees..."

"No one will," he said. "I promise. Come, kiss me again. Little dove. Little Eva."

"I'm not little!"

"No," he said, patting her backside again, "Certainly not. Then come, little dumpling."

She tried to smack him. He grabbed her wrist and brought it to his mouth. Then, smiling wickedly, he kissed her.

She kissed him back. Her trembling lips parted to his claim. He possessed her, filled her, infecting every vein and nerve of her body. Her arms came up around his shoulders and he drove her backwards to the short stone wall. One thigh came up between her legs; he stroked the mound of her pubis lightly, pinning her there...

Her full, ripe breasts swelled against the fabric of her dress. His hands kneaded them, his gaze dropping to the bobbing of her throat. There, under her ear, he planted a kiss that turned into a bite. His fingers brushed her nipples into stiff peaks. Renard's breath grew ragged. Even in her simple village dress Eva LaLaurie could have been fine as any queen, and he felt the urge to claim her descend on him. He began fumbling at her dress.

"You want to do it here?" Eva whispered.

"Yes," he said. "Turn around."

She turned and ruched the edges of her skirt up. He wrapped a hand gently around her throat and pressed into her back. "I love you."

"I love you too."

She heard the undoing of his belt, and then his cock

was sliding against the twin globes of her ass...

She could feel the cream of her arousal running down her leg. He dipped his cock in it, guiding it with his hand...and then he thrust inside her. Impaled, Eva gripped the wall in front of her. Moans of pleasure escaped the confines of Renard's hand, which he had pressed against her lips. He guided his thrusting with a hand on her ass, preventing her from sliding back on it and getting it all to herself.

"Don't move," he whispered. "Darling. Just let me fuck you."

"Oh- Renard..."

And he did. He slid inside her. Each time he brought his cock to her Eva found she was still surprised by his length and girth. He was still a moment so she could get used to him and accept the hot, sturdy pole he thrust into her most secret, intimate place...

Plump as she was, she seemed impossibly small in his

hands. Every part of her, sweeter than honey. He plunged deeper. Breath for breath, movement for movement, they made love in an almost frenzied way. Renard withdrew from her and spun her around to face him. In a single movement he had lifted her in his arms and pinned her against the wall again. His cock resumed its position. Lodged inside her, her ear against his mouth, he whispered words of love, sex words, until he could hear her wetness slicking against his cock and thighs.

"Renard?" came his sister's voice. Eva froze; Renard did not.

"It's alright," he whispered to Eva. "Come for me."

And there they continued, joined in an act of furtive love. Her eyes closed in rapture; she lowered her head to bite into his shoulder.

"Oh Renard...Renard..."

"That's right," he grunted to her. "Say it again, love. I want you to come for me."

And she did.

2

Renard began the painting one fall, when again his mother and sister disappeared for some fete the parish over. The Mauricettes had a second house there, more modest than the first, which his mother and sister were beginning to prefer. It seemed the twenties was to be the age of celebration, for all over Louisiana high society, in the ballrooms that had once hosted antebellum proms over a half-century ago, lavish parties were being thrown. His mother found a new youth in them, and his sister followed, as she always did. Renard guessed his mother had found a new beau among the cavorting masses of the pettishly wealthy. Or perhaps his sister had. Either way, he did not care.

So it was that Renard found the grand Mauricette house empty for much of that September. In such cases he gave all the servants a secret holiday. As he had suspected, the house did not fall to pieces if seven or eight people were not breaking their backs to clean it every day.

Persuading Eva to come up to the house was difficult at first. She seemed in abject terror of it. He did not exactly blame her, but he pressed her all the same.

One night though after much persuading she came up on her own. He let her in through the side door. They snuck upstairs and he pulled a couch out to the high balcony on the third floor. After making love on this couch, not once but several times, they fell asleep intertwined.

He woke before she did and left her sleeping there. He marched into the study and returned with easel, brushes, canvas, and paint. And so when Eva's eyes drifted open she found him, sitting there, absorbed in his work of painting her. In her sleep she had unknowingly struck a kind of *odalisque* pose. She lay partially naked, covered by a thin linen blanket. The rising sun struck her with bars of gold, sending streaks through the brown-black of her hair, and trimming the edges of her dark skin with a burnished copper glow.

"What you doing?" she mumbled sleepily.

"Don't move," he ordered.

Renard worked fast and Renard worked efficiently. He had the shape of her in bold, even strokes. He painted furiously. He chased the light with his brush. Eva fell asleep again, and
when she woke Renard was screwing the caps back on his paints and washing his brushes.

"You done?" asked Eva.

"Yes. Come see."

He turned the canvas towards her. Eva squinted. She

walked over for a closer look.

"Your eyes are bad," Renard observed.

"I know," she sighed. One day they would be about as useful as a chocolate teapot. Moving closer now, she surveyed his hours' work. She breathed deeply.

He had captured her. The very essence of her. Eva had rarely seen art like this- only a few times in her life, in fact. It was called impressionism, Renard told her. But that word didn't mean anything to Eva. So he tried to explain it, which turned into a long lecture which she didn't pay attention to most of. The painting itself enraptured her more than his explanations on art theory.

He seemed to have constructed her out of feathers. That was how she described it to herself later when she tried to picture it again. It was sensuous but yet somehow very innocent. Best of all Renard had not disguised the deep blackness of her skin. Nor the tight coils of her hair. A single breast lay modestly exposed, and the blanket hid the rest. Eva's throat closed.

"Paintin's got to have a name," she said.

"I call it *innocence*," replied Renard.

And innocence it was. It was a love letter. Unmistakably.

"What you going to do with it?" she asked.

"Leave it here," said Renard. "And one day frame it."

"And no one will see it."

"They won't. No one ever comes up here."

"You gonna sell it?"

"No."

But he did cover the canvas and move it into the

corner, under the awning and away from the rain. And he led Eva back inside.

For some reason when they parted that afternoon for Renard to run some errands over the river, Eva was left with an unpleasant feeling she could not shake. He kissed her, stroked her hair. She kissed him back and wrapped her arms tightly around him.

"I'll come again tonight?"

"Yes," she said. She wanted to see him, but still...

He kissed her again and gave her a sudden, tight squeeze. She laughed and bussed another kiss against his cheek. Then, leaning on the cane he no longer seemed to need, he strolled away. Eva watched his tall figure recede into the distance. Whenever they parted she always wondered if it might be the last time. Anything could happen. This thing they were building between them was as fragile as a spider's lace.

All her doubts and fears that built up when he was

away always disappeared immediately the next time she saw him. She would just have to wait.

Someone hailed her down the path- Nelson. Eva was glad to be pulled from her spiraling thoughts. She raised her arm in greeting. The old Indian padded over to her, his face wrinkled in a rare smile.

"Hiya, Evie," he said. "Where you comin' from?"

"The erm, the Mauricette place," said Eva, knowing it was useless to lie.

"Alright," said Nelson smoothly. He patted the knife at his waist and winked at her. "Everythin' okay? Or I need to teach someone a lesson?"

"I'm alright," she laughed. She eyed the man. Dark circles ringed under his eyes- he looked like he hadn't slept in days.

Sometimes Nelson took draughts for insomnia. He didn't need Evie to make these and he picked the herbs himself. Sometimes they helped. Sometimes they didn't. It took a lot to silence the old man's demons.

Eva knew very little about Nelson's early life. She supposed there was a time when he hadn't lived in Rue Cher. Before then he had a place somewhere out in the swamp and he lived there with his son. Then his son went to war and came back and blew his brains out with his own gun. Nelson moved to Rue Cher a short time after.

Eva's affection for the man was bottomless. He called her daughter.

"You ain't been sleepin'," she said.

"I know it," he replied. "Need some of the white people stuff. That morphine."

She knew better than to ask him outright what was wrong. He would eventually tell her. In his usual roundabout way.

"Been seein' that Tom feller," he began. "Helped fix his door."

Eva had heard about what folks were now calling the Shanter Incident. Three white men had gone and nearly burned Shanter's wife and children up to cinders to make him sign over his land. Luckily Tom had friends in the right places, and they reinstated his deed papers in a hurry, just in case the white men tried to forge his signature. Still, if Esau and Nelson hadn't intervened that afternoon... She shivered. "You think they gonna come back?"□

"Sure as the moon rises," said Nelson. "Ain't a question of if, but when."

"What we gonna do?"

"Hell if I know," said Nelson. "Same as we always do, I reckon. Cope. We all been tellin' Tom to split for the winter. But he's 'fraid they gonna burn the house up while he's gone. And besides the girls can't go nowhere, with school startin' up."

"Lord have mercy."

"Hmmph," snorted Nelson. "The more time that goes on, the more crickety I get. Ain't just Tom we got to worry about. It's gonna be all of us in the fire if we dont do somethin'."

"No doubt," said Eva. She now wished Nelson would stop talking. Talk about something else. The reverie of her time with Renard that morning had all but evaporated. She was left with that sinking feeling again- but worse.

Nelson continued, "I got prospectors of my own comin' my way now. A man. And a white lady."

"A white woman?"

"Yep," said Nelson. And now he looked at Eva from the tail of his eye.

"Got long black hair. Lot of jewelry. Came by last night, matter of fact."

"Oh- Nelson."

"Scary lookin' bitch," he said, and spat.

"Oh Lord. I got a bad feelin' about this."

"You know, Evie, I been thinkin'," said Nelson, in a different tone of voice. "You know how the old folks say you can feel when your time is comin' up?"

Nelson was "old folks" to Eva, but she nodded, agreeing. "They do say that," she said cautiously. "Why? You feelin' that way?"

"Oh, yeah," said Nelson. He nodded and closed his eyes, breathing deeply. "I think about how you always told me that stuff is livin' and dyin' all in a big circle," he said. "I agree, you know. I think maybe Rue Cher's done wore out its welcome in this world. And now we got to die and go somewhere else. Just another

229

circle we movin' around."

"I don't want to think that," said Eva. The very idea made her want to cry.

"I feelin' the same way about m'self. Like I got to move on somewhere else."

"Back to Georgia, you mean?" asked Eva. Nelson had always used to talk about going back to Georgia.

"Naw," he said. "Just, you know, dying."

"Oh, Nelson."

"When I die," said Nelson, his eyes twinkling mischievously, "I want to come back as a 'gator."

"What for?" laughed Eva.

"They just lay in the mud and look tough. Don't nobody mess with a gator. Except probably an Indian. I'm gonna come back and take a big bite out of someone's behind if they try messin' with me. Indian or no."

Eva giggled helplessly. Then they walked in silence for some time, until Eva turned to him again.

"You know about me and Renard?"

A wry smile twisted on his face. "Seems 'bout the whole village knows about you and that rich son of a bitch. Folks ain't too happy about it."

This was not a surprise. "What they sayin'?"

"Same old shit," he said vaguely. Nelson was not one to carry gossip. "They want you to settle with someone from Rue Cher. One of your own. But you's you, Evie. You always gonna do what you want. I just want you to be careful."

"I'm bein' careful," she said, knowing that she was not.

They reached the fork in the road. "Meetin' today," were his parting words. "Mitch Davis's place, noon. We gonna talk about what to do about all this."

"Bye, Nelson."

"Bye, daughter."

Renard was supposed to be coming later...But no matter. Eva resolved to go to the gathering. Her conversation with Nelson had served as a brutal reminder that there was more going on in Rue Cher that overshadowed her love affair. Things she owed more attention to.

♞

Renard Mauricette came home from over the river. He had a large package in his hand which was to be a gift for Eva. Renard had long guessed Eva's intrigue at the idea of becoming a doctor. With this gift he hoped to encourage her. He planned to stop at home and refresh himself before heading down the river to see her, as promised, and deliver her the present.

But when Renard arrived at the gates of the Mauricette place he found Amelie Mordant, and Louis Mordant, and Constable Taylor, waiting for him. His mother and sister stood aside putting on a great display of weeping.

Renard stopped.

"What's this?"

"You are under arrest, Monsieur," said the constable warily. He looked very much like he would rather be anywhere else. "For assault and kidnapping."

"Kidnapping," said Renard. He tied Eva's package to his saddle. "And who did I kidnap?"

"Come on, now," said Constable Taylor wearily.

"Our son," sobbed Amelie. "Oh Renard- how could

you?"

"I have no son," said Renard, still caught up by the strange humor of the situation. He perceived the truth at once. "But I would not hurt an innocent child. This woman is lying, Taylor. You can see she is good at it. Lots of practice."

"Watch your tongue," warned Louis Mordant.

"I will not," snapped Renard. "This is an affront to justice."

"My poor child," said Amelie. "So alone in the dark."

"A sorry business," agreed Taylor feebly.

"You would hurt a child to get to me," said Renard, astonished. Though of course that was not half of what he knew her capable of. Amelie had once told him she had held a servant girl's arm over a cooking fire for burning her dress while ironing. He put nothing past her.

"Arrest this worm," snarled Louis. "I will not have my lamb's honor questioned. By her husband, no less-"

"Ex-husband," Amelie couldn't help adding. She gave a piteous sniff. "He dishonors me with every breath."

This seemed to solidify something in the constable's mind, and he nodded. "Right. Monsieur, I am afraid we must take you in. Just for the night- you understand- you will have a lawyer, of course..." afraid to anger the Mauricettes, who were an important and honored family, but also needing to pacify the Mordants, who financially controlled the parish, Constable Taylor found himself in a bind. He made a grab at Renard's wrists, but the taller man snatched them away.

"Absolutely not," he said, outraged. "You have no proof."

"The boy was found in your cellar, Monsieur," said Taylor helplessly. "You ordered the servants away. You been seen wanderin' up and down, disappearin' at night...And your opinion of the boy is less than favorable. Your own mother said so. Given the evidence..."

"And how did you discover a small child in the cellar," demanded Renard, "when I had ordered the servants away, as you just said? Have I invisible spies in my own house? Did the cutlery walk to the station and deliver a report?" He was struck by the ludicrousness of what he'd said. Of the whole operation. He quelled the urge towards laughter, which would only cement his guilt.

"An anonymous tip," supplied Louis, his eyebrows lowering dangerously. "Why should it matter? You are guilty, and there is proof."

"Please, Monsieur," begged Constable Taylor. He himself was unsure of the law in these cases- a man could not kidnap his own son, after all. And surely it was not illegal to punish a little boy by locking him up somewhere for a bit. He had a very correct suspicion that this was all a setup by the Mordants and they were playing on his ignorance. But still. Louis Mordant could easily have him out of a job- and had threatened as much.

"You will have to beat me to this earth before I spend a night in jail," declared Renard. He rounded on Taylor and slammed a fist to his own breast. "After all this family has done for you. My father himself gave you that post-"

"I must take you in," said the Constable doggedly. "No one is above the law."

"Then by all means do your best," replied Renard. He reached for his pistol. Madame Mauricette shrieked. But Taylor was faster. He had his own gun out, but his expression was contrite.

"Don't make this ugly, Monsieur," cringed Taylor. "I got to put you in for a night. But shoot that thing off and you'll be looking at a month, at least."

"I won't. I refuse."

"No apologies!" said Louis, outraged. "Have some backbone, man!"

Fiona Mauricette's sudden gasp broke through the tension. She shrieked and pointed. "Good Heavenly Lord! What's that?"

A column of smoke- thick, black smoke, was rising down the hill.

"Oh," said Amelie, sounding strangely delighted. "Oh my."

They followed the cloud to the red glow of its source. Fire, fire. Rue Cher was on fire.

Several minutes before Renard faced the confrontation, Eva LaLaurie sat in the crowded church of Rue Cher, nursing a massive headache.

It was the first meeting since the Shanter Incident, and everyone was rightly incensed. It seemed Charles St. Joseph had been busier than the devil. Almost everyone had received some kind of threat or intimidation.

The gathering had divided into two camps. Those in favor of staying in Rue Cher and weathering out the white folks, and those in favor of leaving.

"We ought to leave," said Esau LaLaurie. "Go North. Almost everyone else is doin' it."

"Stronger together," insisted Tom. "And I'm sayin' that. And I got more cause to leave than any of y'all. If we all start runnin' for the hills, we gonna leave a lot of folks here helpless."

"We helpless right now," retorted Sarie Jules, the only

woman with a loud enough voice to cut above the mens' shouting. "How many guns we got? And even if we barricaded ourselves in here and held 'em out, you think talk of a negro army out in Rue Cher ain't gonna bring the hoods and torches like ants to sugar? Pshaw. They gonna cross state lines to put us down."

"We defendin' what's ours, Sarie," said Tom, rounding on his old enemy.

"Naw, y'all bein' big and bold and actin' like you got none of the sense your momma gave you. Think about your wife, them little girls. You puttin' their necks out for your pride."

"Just like a woman to want to cut and run," said Tom derisively.

"A loud mouth makes a soft ass, Shanter!"

The church rang with arguing. "Hey now," said Esau LaLaurie, trying to mediate. "We came here to talk it out, not argue like a pack of geese. Let's hear from someone else."

"We don't even know if the crackers gonna come after us anyway," piped up Chillo. "And y'all keep talkin' bout movin' up to Detroit like you so sure the white folks there gonna be any better." He paused. "Y'all can't even spell Detroit."

That broke them all up, but then they were back to the start. Exhausted, Eva rested her head against the pew and looked at the worm-eaten ceiling. A symbolic thing to notice, that. They'd been talking about fixing the church roof for ages. But as was the case with many things in Rue Cher, talk would only ever be talk unless something else forced them into action.

They would talk in circles around the issue until the threat went away or the white folks attacked straight up. Little did Eva know that tonight every hand in Rue Cher would be forced towards its own decision.

The argument was proceeding in its usual direction-that is, circular- when the church door banged open. They fell silent immediately. Little Anastasie Shanter stood in the doorway.

"Come quick!" she screeched. "They burnin' Mama's house!"

They piled out of the church in one mass, and scattered.

Eva and Nelson raced off together. They lived closest to Tom and to each other. And Nelson had a gun.

The night had descended in a thick cloak of darkness, but the burning of Tom Shanter's cabin served as a soft, sinister light. Through the winding paths they tumbled, spurred by their fear. It took them ten minutes to cross over to their place, but by then it was too late. A small crowd of armed white men were outside Eva's cabin. Some wore hoods, but most had not bothered. Eva gasped. Nelson pulled her into the tree line. Luckily the men were too occupied with digging out Eva's house to notice.

"Don't make a sound," muttered Nelson. "I'm gonna run back for my rifle."

"Don't leave me!" she begged, but he was already gone.

She had no choice but to watch the men toss out all her belongings in the garden. Her eyesight, usually not the greatest, still gave her the general idea. All of it was tipped out the door. Even the bed. All her herbs. Her medicine bottles, so hard won and meticulously collected, they smashed to pieces. For a dizzying moment she thought of Renard's ring- but then remembered it was in her pocket. She didn't start to cry until they got to her books. Renard had found these for her- no one else in Rue Cher had the means to get books. They had been an object of interest for anyone who came through her door. Foolishly, she had left them all out on display. These seemed to confuse the mob- then it made them angry. Someone poured something over the pile of stuff in her garden. And Eva LaLaurie watched her life's work go up in flames.

Naturally, the cabin her grandfather had built was next. They lit this carelessly. And then she had to bury her face in her skirts. She couldn't bear to look.

The white mob moved with brutal efficiency. They swept across Rue Cher in a wave, torching whatever they could find. The dry weather of the last few weeks had turned the wood to tinder. The torches worked quickly.

Nelson found his cabin already in smoke, with his rifle inside it. The mob was nowhere to be seen, but he could hear yells and shouting over the small ridge. Sparks swirled in the air like red hot snow crystals. He stared at the sight of his burning cabin for a minute, then doubled back through the trees. The night came alive around him; the wild animals, spooked by the smoke, were on edge. They had not decided on whether to get moving. He ran on the balls of his feet, hardly making a sound.

When he got to Esau's, he first saw the man stationed in front of his house with his shotgun. Nelson supposed Esau's wife and son had fled into the swamp with the others. The black man's face was drawn and frightened. He nearly shot Nelson to death as he approached.

"Jesus Christ," said Esau.

"They got Eva's place," said Nelson. "You should leave, or you gonna be next. Looks like they're torchin' the whole edge of the village."

"I won't," said Esau. "They got to kill me first."

"No use dyin' over a house. You can rebuild the house."

"It's the principle," said Esau. "A man's got to defend his property. It's my right." His voice shook.

"I'm goin' to the constable," said Nelson. He meant the police station over the river. "You should come."

Esau gave a harsh, dry bark. Nelson could risk his neck at the white man's police station all he wanted. He wasn't budging.

"You think these police give a rat's ass about this? I seen one of 'em lightin' the fires myself."

Nelson had to agree. In the end the two of them made their way to the forest again. Nelson wanted to check on Eva.

They did not find Eva. They did, however, find a group that had detached from the white mob.

The group had doubled back to the forest, taking a break from the festivities of burning and looting. A small campfire roasted merrily between them. Nelson and Esau, in their panicked hurry, stumbled right into these men, thinking they were folks from Rue Cher. They were, technically speaking, from Rue Cher. Just the wrong side of Rue Cher. The men had a dog on a rawhide leash. And every single one of them was armed. Nelson and Esau might have been two elephants crashing into their little camp. They were noticed immediately.

"Hell and shit," said Esau.

"Well," said one of the white men. This was Charles St. Joseph. A tall, thin man in a suit sat on a log next to him. The lantern this man held aloft illuminated the faces of the other two, and three discarded white hoods at their feet. Charles smiled through a clot of tobacco leaves, and spat. "Lookee-here."

"We ain't come for trouble," said Esau. He gripped his shotgun. An old, rusty thing that hardly shot straight.

"Neither did we, nigger," said Charles St. Joseph. He got to his feet, and so did his companions. "But it seems like y'all is trespassin', anyhow."

"These is our woods," said Esau. "Bought and paid for."

They advanced; Nelson and Esau retreated.

"Not for long. Now say why I shouldn't string you from that tree?"

" 'Cause it's against the law," said Nelson, with an odd humor jumping under the words. St. Joseph was not amused. Neither was Esau; he glared at the old Indian furiously.

"This is the white man's country," spoke the tall thin man. "And white men make the laws."

"That's right," agreed Charles. He reached for a long, heavy club resting against the log. "And now I'm feelin' to turn both your guts to garters. Y'all high-steppin' bastards can be the example we need to turn the rest out and get this land in good folks' hands."

"We just gonna head on back," said Esau, backing up. "You right. These is your woods."

"I don't think so," sneered another man. "Looks like y'all came hankerin' for a fight." He jutted his chin at Esau's gun and gripped his pistol. "You want a fight with us?"

"No," said Esau. "No, thank you."

"Run," suggested Nelson.

They ran.

♘

The men in hoods spread across the small plains of Rue Cher like a disease, ravaging in a single night what had taken generations to build.

But the sun still rose over all the mess. Somehow. It is the nature of the world to always bring on another day. No matter the wretchedness of the night before. Somehow the sun rises.

That was what Eva thought when she woke up, covered in leaves and soot, to face the sudden horror her life had become. She had not been dreaming, though it was a miracle that she had even fallen asleep. Her legs and arms were covered in bites she scarcely felt. She realized, dimly, that had the fire spread to the line of trees at any other point in the village she likely would have been incinerated.

Eva rolled out of the thicket and made the short walk to the ruins of her house. The cottage of her grandmother, grandfather and mother was now a pile of ashes. The ash-pile smelled like burned grease. Broken glass littered all over the ruins of her yard. Her plants were torn up and the old dogwood tree was a charred skeleton. Pathetic trails of smoke rose from the blackened foundation. The house had burned all night, burned itself out.

She picked through the wreckage, as many others in Rue Cher were doing. Not much had been left. And she felt nothing. There was nothing to feel.

Was this her village? Could it be the same place that a day before had been so green and beautiful? No; no it could never be.

She knew that folks might need her around Rue Cher to do doctoring and mending and healing. But for now Eva was too tired. And she feared the news these other folks would bring. If she stayed right here she could pretend it had only been her house that had been ruined. She could pretend everyone else was fine. Soot choked her lungs and heart.

She sat down in the wreckage of her cabin and put her head on her knees. Too dried up to cry, she waited for the morning to unfold.

In time the reporters would come, and then the folks from a ways over, curious to see the carnage. In time the folks of Rue Cher would take an account of their numbers and ask around for the dead. Not all houses had been burned; indeed very many remained intact. But the message was clear: they needed to leave.

Now.

The houses targeted for burning had not been at random. Eva, Nelson and Tom all bordered the edge of Rue Cher. They were all, in some way, pillars of the community.

As Rue Cher sagged under the weight of the previous night, Renard Mauricette lay in a cell in the local prison. He sat in the corner, his leg stretched out stiffly in front of him. True to his word Constable Taylor intended to let the Mauricette out of jail that afternoon. But Renard was convinced that he would remain at least till the next weekend. He was the only person in the cell.

Rumors of what had happened that night came into the station in bursts. He strained to listen. Some said they had burned down all the negro houses. Some said they hung six men. Some said it was just two. The police made all sorts of guesses of their own and they seemed to think the whole affair rather amusing. They discussed it that morning over a bottle of whisky and a card game.

By the time Constable Taylor put key to lock and let the ruffled Mauricette out, Renard's temper had billowed into a rolling fury. He ignored the constable's bleating apologies and requests to not let Louis know he had released him. Renard collected his hat and limped out of the courthouse with death in his heart.

He did not make it far before the very last person he wanted to see turned up. Amelie Mordant was waiting outside. She held a cigarette in a gloved hand.

"Hello Renard," she said.

"Come any closer," said Renard brutally, "And you'll get a nice bruise to go with that dress."

"Not using your cane, I see?" she chirped. "A pity. You look so dashing with it."

The woman wore a scarlet dress that brought out the

olive undertones of her skin. Her hair had been done up in an elaborate top knot. An emerald, suspended from a silver chain, hung at her throat. Overdressed, in her usual sinister way.

"How do I look?" she said, running a hand down her torso.

"Like the devil's wife."

"Watch your tongue," said Amelie. She smirked. "You are speaking to the richest woman in Rue Cher."

"Indeed?" said Renard. "An honor I do not deserve. Good day."

"You will find," said Amelie, ashing her cigarette and hurrying to keep up with him, "That your negro pets won't be around any longer to distract you. Last night Papa acquired six of their properties. Sold to him right on the spot. For pennies, in fact." She tinkled a laugh. "I heard they burnt your wench's house to cinders- my request. Unfortunately she was not inside."

Renard turned suddenly and grabbed her. Her eyes flew wide in surprise. Never had he turned on her physically. He jerked her towards him, and she stumbled. Later on she would peel back her sleeve and see four dark bruises on the shoulder.

A couple walked past them and gasped, scandalized.

"It's alright," gritted Renard at them through a horrible leer, "Just a marital dispute."

The couple ducked their heads and hurried on.

"Brute," panted Amelie. She was trying to smile; act unbothered. But it rang false; he had truly frightened her. Good.

"Tell me what you want from me," he said.

Her eyes sparkled. "To ruin you, Renard. That's what

I want."

"And why?"

"Because," she said, "I am so horribly bored."

It was what he had known for years. Amelie didn't need a reason for her cruelty. She enjoyed tormenting people and she fixated on people, things, creatures, to tear apart a piece at a time. Renard had just been her unfortunate victim. He released her. A taste like old copper was in his mouth. He spat it at her feet.

"It is a shame that a woman like you became a mother."

"Not for long," said Amelie, dusting off her skirts. "I'm ridding myself of the brat as soon as possible."

He stared at her, shocked. "Even you would not murder an innocent child. Lock him in a cellar, maybe-"

"You have so little faith in me. You have no idea what I would do."

Renard had never even seen Amelie's little boy. The child's name was Henri Christoff or something like that. Even if he was a bastard, and the son of this witch, in his heart Renard could feel nothing but pity for the child. His legal son. He feared that if he ever laid eyes on the boy he might be immediately tempted to whisk him away from his vulture of a mother.

It would have been the right thing to do from the beginning, but Renard had been a coward. He'd thought he had enough to worry about. Now he was began to have serious doubts. Could he let an innocent child be preyed on by Amelie Mordant?

No, he could not.

"I am going to get that child out of your clutches," he told her.

"Good luck," said the woman. "He is legally my

property. They would not separate a mother and child."

Renard fell silent on that point. He meant what he said- he had to get the boy away from that woman as soon as possible. But it was best not to goad her further. Best to let her think she had won. "Then I wish you every happiness," he told her, and turned away.

"Loyalties run deep in this part of the country," she said quickly, determined to get the last word. "The constable wouldn't think of holding you another night. Even when I threatened him. But you haven't seen the last of me, Renard."

"Unfortunately."

He ignored her and she eventually went away, like a bored cat.

The first thing he did was go straight to Rue Cher. He smelled the little village before he saw it. And before he walked down the knoll to investigate, he took a deep breath and had a moment to think.

Of course, his thoughts turned back to Eva.

CHAPTER SEVEN

The land of Rue Cher was desirable, because the land of Rue Cher was beautiful. The forest. The swamp, the marshes, the river. They rolled on through and they were full of secrets, secrets older than the thoughts of men.

It was in the nature of the society of the men to want to carve up the pieces of earth and lay claim to it. Because in this world, a man's wealth was all he hand. Money could pass through hands like water. Money could come and go like the wind. But land? Ah. Land was eternal, wasn't it? And if you claimed the land, then you could be eternal too.

But all land had a price, and the price was usually blood.

East Rue Cher had been purchased with blood. But not the blood of the conqueror or the coward or the cheat. It had been bought by people who went to sleep with sore backs and howling stomachs.

That was a long time ago, and these were not very happy people. They had hope they would someday be happy and they worked for that to happen. Sometimes work was not enough. But those that survived and hauled themselves out tooth and nail were able to buy their piece of earth and put their name upon it. And now, with the darkness lifted like a veil from their eyes they saw they could help others, and they reached back in to the pit they had come from and pulled their brothers and sisters out. They understood that they had not struggled in vain. For the reward of their labor (a reward sweeter because they shared it with those who knew their struggle) was a piece of eternity, the land of Rue Cher itself.

They were not its owners, but its protectors and defenders. And these folks died easy knowing their children would not have to suffer as they had- to the extent they had. For the land would surely protect them, too.

As the descendants of these people picked through the wreckage of their homes, as word came of those who had fled and given up their land, of two men found hanging from an oak tree in the forest, of a child missing, a woman raped, the weight of the whole injustice settled heavily on the shoulders of the people of Rue Cher.

Many realized that holding on to their piece of the world demanded too great a price. They had been taxed too much. It was the final straw. So they began to pack up and leave.

It was into this madness that Renard Mauricette stumbled that afternoon, coming back from the Rue Cher station.

"Renard?"

"Yes, it's me."

Eva picked herself up out of the ashes. Her dress was caked in soot, and she was barefoot. Gray streaked the dark, smooth skin of her face.

To Renard she seemed like a creature of some other world. Almost like a ghost.

"Are you alright?" he asked, hesitantly. He realized this was a stupid question. Of course she was not alright.

"I'm still here," she said. "So I must be."

The viciousness of what had happened was almost incomprehensible. Eva's beautiful little cabin was now a mound of hideous cinders. Even the air surrounding them was foul. She crawled out of it almost pathetically. And she seemed shrunken somehow. He was afraid to touch her.

"Where were you?" she asked tonelessly. "I thought you might come do something."

She did not sound angry with him- merely disgusted. As if he had lived up to her expectations.

"I was in jail," he told her. The excuse sounded too ludicrous to be believed, even to his ears. "They put me there right before I saw it burning."

She fixed him with a stare, black and cold and full of hatred. "Did you know?"

"Eva," he said, simply. "Of course I didn't know. I swear."

But in a way, he had. He recalled that meeting with Charles and Broglie oh-so-long ago. There are other ways to force niggers off land...quicker ways. And he had let them shanty right out of his study. Telling himself naively that they wouldn't dare. Whereupon they had dared.

He was to blame, too. For knowing, and doing nothing.

"They got Nelson," she said. "And my cousin. They hung 'em from a tree." Her lips trembled but she did not cry.

"I'm so sorry," he said.

"Nelson never hurt nobody," she said, in a small voice. "Esau was a good man. H-had a family, too."

And then she was crying in earnest, and she didn't step into the arms he held out to her, but sank to her knees and curled up on herself.

Renard knelt next to her. He took her into his arms,

awkwardly, in the way of a man unused to giving others comfort. Eva did not resist him. But then she pulled away and fumbled in her dress. The opal ring lay nested in her palm.

"Take it back," she said. Her red-rimmed eyes were determined. "It's no good to me."

He looked at the small bauble, and its uselessness seemed magnified in the scope of what surrounded them. What did a ring matter- and what did a ring prove? It was nothing for Renard to give Eva something like that. He could have thrown pretty presents at her feet all the livelong day. But it would not be enough.

Did he love Eva? Yes, he did. He loved her because she was a good woman, because she was beautiful, funny, intelligent. Eva deserved better than his scraps. Eva deserved better than a pile of ashes. Eva deserved the world.

"Keep it," he told her. She shook her head, but he

pulled her to her feet.

"Listen here," he said. "I will do something about what happened. I will make it right."

"You can't," she said, wiping her eyes. "Nobody's expectin' you to."

He looked around. "Where are you sleeping tonight?"

She sniffed and scrubbed the heel of her hand across her eyes. "Probably with Sam's Momma, if she got room."

"Come up to the house with me."

"No, Renard," she said. "I can't just cut and run."

He shook his head and chucked her under the chin. "I wish you would do the wrong thing for once."

"Never," she said with a choked laugh. "I'm born to be a goody-good."

They got up and walked around some more. Eva led him to the shell of Nelson's cabin and they poked through the smoking embers together. Renard took stock of everything he saw. Eva was looking for a keepsake of Nelson, but she found nothing. Like her house, all of its contents had been reduced to dust.

"People ought to hear about this," he said, when they left. "Other people. The whole country."

"Reporters came 'round here this morning, askin' questions. I don't think they liked what folks had to say."

"They will mangle the truth, of course."

"Don't I know it?" said Eva. "But ain't nothin' new."

In the end it was Renard, not Eva, who wrote the newspaper article on the sacking of Rue Cher. He wrote it in a day. It was as honest and true account as he could make it. Only a few people had agreed to speak with him, and only at Eva's insistence.

Then other Negro reporters came from areas of the state, educated folks from the colleges and cities, and they wrote about it too. They wrote passionate pleas to the northern humanitarian societies, the Governor, even President Harding. They wrote articles and essays. It all amounted to very little.

Though Renard asked, Eva insisted it would not be a wise idea to show his face around the village for a while. Everyone knew that it was the Mordants and their henchmen who had started the burning. But it was the Mauricettes they blamed. For surely the Mauricettes, meaning Renard, ought to have known about the attack and given warning. And if Renard was so close with Eva, then why did he let this happen?

Renard stayed out of their way. Every day he went down to spend time with Eva. But every night he returned home, his heart heavy.

On one of these nights he returned in a particularly nasty temper. Eva's mood was not improving. They were getting into heated fights. He kept asking her to leave; she was refusing. He learned she had sold the Opal ring to pay someone else's passage up North. Renard understood the sentiment, but she had not told him, and it seemed like a rejection. If Eva wanted money all she had to do was ask him.

But she had returned his matter-of-fact statement with barbed words and veiled accusations. And Renard had said some unkind things. They did not part on easy terms.

So he sat down to dinner with his small family that night in a black temper. As usual, the presence of his mother and idiot sister only made it worse.

"You've been going down to the village again."

"Yes."

"Why?"

"To lend assistance."

"You disappoint me, Renard."

"I do not care, Mother."

"I don't know what you're complaining about, Renard. The sooner these vermin are gone, the better. Your grandfather should have never sold them that damned land in the first place. What a waste."

"And where will the people living there go now?"

"To hell. Perhaps back to Africa."

"This is their home. Have you no sympathy?"

"I? Sympathy?" barked the old woman. "Who ever had sympathy for negroes?"

"And you call yourself a Christian?" fired back Renard.

"I am a child of God. And you are a disgrace to the family," said his mother.

"This family had no honor to begin with."

"Then get out!" she huffed. "The son of a sodomite turned into a nigger-lover. What a family I married into." And she turned moodily back to her pastry.

Renard looked at his mother from across the parlor table with new eyes. He could not summon an ounce of affection for her. He never had been able to. The damned old shrew. She was picking at her food. Her squat frame was stuffed into tight, old-fashioned clothes. Any outward beauty had long ago fled. Her face was blotchy from the spurious moments of temper, and her mouth pursed on itself like a dog's bottom. She had never had anything nice to say in her life and it showed.

His sister sat simpering at Madame's elbow. More of a lapdog than a daughter. Renard always pitied her until she opened her mouth. Then she could be just as callous as her mother. Indeed, Fiona was looking more like the old harpy every day.

Because they were his family, and because he had once put his honor and duty before everything, Renard had been forgiving of their abrasive presence at the main house. Or at least he had tolerated it. But his tolerance had abruptly ended.

They lounged about and did nothing but spend the Mauricette inheritance on extravagant things. They hit the servants and had fits of temper for attention. What they said about the poor folks down in Rue Cher made him seethe with disgust.

Moreover, they cared for him not at all. As a child they had ignored him; as an adult they had scorned him while leeching off his labor of keeping the family afloat. And they were sorry he had not spent longer in prison. He knew for certain they would have been quite happy if he had died in the war, for then they might have found another man's patience to leech on.

They said blood was thicker than water. Yes; and blood would choke you if you didn't spit it out.

"That's it," he said, standing abruptly.

"That's what?" snarled his mother. "Sit down, Renard. You're shaking the table."

He did more than shake the table. He stepped back and took a hold of the tablecloth. He gave a pull and sent all the fine 19th century China shattering to the floor. And then he flipped the whole thing over, unfortunately just missing their toes.

Madame emitted a mighty screech and got to her feet. With perfect timing, Fiona began to cry.

"You are finished," said Renard. "I demand you get out of this house."

"With what authority?" shrieked Madame.

"With my own. This house is mine in deed and title. Leave, or I'll throw you out myself."

"Renard," wailed Fiona, "How could you?"

Was he being heartless? He opened his mouth to change his mind, but in the end said nothing. Renard had been the sole inheritor of Gaspard's property and fortune. It was his house, legally. Let her see how it felt to be thrown out of her own home.

"I will not leave!" declared his mother.

Renard feinted towards her, and all the fight went out of her when he did. Clearly enough of Gaspard had showed on his face to frighten her.

"Come, Fiona!" she said. She stormed from the room, her witless daughter scurrying after her. In a trice she had a bag packed and was hauling Fiona down the stairs. She slammed out the front door and shouted for a carriage, which was brought. Renard waited until they were gone. He supposed they would go to the

Mauricette's second home.

In any case Renard now had what he wanted, which was peace and quiet for the next few days. He set to work on his plan.

♘

"You sellin' the house?" said Eva. She couldn't believe it.

"Yes," he said. "But I must take care of some things first."

Eva still wore the same dress she'd had on the night of the fire. She looked bedraggled and sleep deprived. Nelson and Esau's funerals had been that morning. She hadn't anything nice to put on but a clean kerchief.

When Renard met her at the entrance to Rue Cher

and saw her state he knew he had to put his foot down. Since their unpleasant parting earlier Eva looked even worse than she had been. Her eyes were sunken and drawn, like she hadn't slept.

"You are coming with me," he said.

"I can't," she said.

"Indeed you are. We should talk."

She looked angry at his demands, but then her face softened. "I'm sorry, Renard. For how I've been acting."

"I think, Eva, the apology should be mine. But don't distract me. I want you to come home with me."

"They publish your article yet?"

Renard had submitted his piece to almost every local publication he could think of. Even The Daily Item all the way down in New Orleans. No one wanted the story. He received only one letter back, calling the piece "incendiary and strongly-worded."

He told Eva about it. She clicked her teeth. Then she refused his offer to come visit again. But in the end she agreed. He suspected, correctly, that she was tired of being cramped into a cabin with five other people.

When she arrived at the Mauricette house, Renard had not dismissed the staff. They still wandered about pretending to look busy. Most had figured out that Renard did not particularly care if they did a little idling. They were not happy to see Eva. Though they worked for the Mauricettes, they were still people of Rue Cher. And her attachment to Renard displeased them. They gave her some looks that said: I hope you don't think you better than us, now.

Once upstairs Eva took the filthy dress off and sank into the bath Renard had drawn for her. Immediately she forgot everything. The troubles of before melted away. Renard poured a delicious smelling soap in with the water and Eva scrubbed herself from head to toe.

All her life bathing had been a freezing, furtive thing. Now she lay back and let the water and sweet smell of lavender and juniper consume her. She wished the bath could be even hotter. Oh, this was what luxury felt like. Her eyes opened on to another vaulted ceiling, but there were no white cherubs and angels staring down at her; only roses. The rose was the symbol of the Mauricette family.

Renard had a fluffy towel waiting for her when she emerged, queen-like and dripping. This he wrapped around her entire frame. She sat on the fine feather bed while he dried her back and hair.

"I have a plan for us," he said. "And you just got to let me talk. No interrupting."

"Alright, Renard."

"We're going to get married," he began, and Eva started.

"Hey now," warned Renard. "You're gonna let me finish."

"Crazy-talk."

He dug his fingers into her sides, tickling her, and she squealed and batted at his hands.

"I'm serious. No funny stuff. We're going to do it proper," he said.

"It's against the law!"

"In Louisiana, yes. But as I see it, we don't need to be in Louisiana to get married."

She looked at him. He wasn't joking.

"Renard, I don't know if I believe this."

"Why not?"

"Dear life. You are serious."

"I'm always serious," he said, "when it comes to you."

"Where will we go?"

"Boston," he answered immediately. "I have a place there."

Would Boston be a little more accepting of their circumstance? Perhaps. But perhaps not. In fact, it was very likely that no matter where they went they would be shunned. Eva's people would think she was a disgrace. Renard's people would think he was even worse.

But who were Eva's 'people' now? The folks of Rue Cher- now running and scattering to the winds. Soon she wouldn't have a people to think of. Soon they would all be gone.

As for Renard and his place in white society...well. That was his concern. He was always telling her he had enough money to do whatever he wanted. She supposed he was going to prove it to her.

Eva put aside her worries of the future. Her man had laid down the towel and was kissing up her neck. Yes, She had Renard. Renard was more real than anything else. And he was here, willing to lay his fortune on the line for her.

He wants to marry me! She turned around and jumped on him. He fell to the bed in a heap of laughter. It was the happiest she had felt in days. Weeks, even. She decided to put the sadness of the last few days to the side. Just for the moment.

He wrapped her in his arms and rolled her underneath him.

"Now," he said, "What would you like for dinner?"

"You," she giggled, her hands skimming down his stomach to cup the hardness stirring in his trousers. Renard's eyebrows raised.

"Oh?"

That night some unknown force woke Renard from sleep. Eva was curled up next to him in the shelter of his arms. They were naked.

Renard tried to fall asleep again but could not. So he rose up and put on some modest clothes and went to have a cigarette outside. He kissed her cheek and patted her bottom and crept out of the room.

Eva, feeling him wake but saying nothing, got up herself. She followed him out of the room.

At the landing of the main staircase Renard lit a match to the greasy parrafin lamp he had left on the foyer table that afternoon. Eva waited for him to turn the corner before she continued.

He had decided to take a night tour of the place

instead of smoking, hoping to ease his nerves. Renard wound his way past the portraits of his ancestors. He would be glad to sell them along with the house. They all looked like different versions of his father. Unpleasant, fat, lazy. He was ashamed of them.

He passed the cabinets of fine China, the acres of brocade curtains hanging in the drawing room. The gild-bronzed ceiling, painted with creatures of pale and smiling innocence. In the greasy light they looked like ghouls.

Moving outdoors into the kitchens the comforts of home seemed more apparent, because his family had rarely entered here. The cellar door loomed eerily in the corner. He remembered with a smile how the servants had conspired to lock Amelie in the cellar.

As if to lure him, he swore he heard a sound coming from its depths. In truth, it was only an underground breeze. But it sounded like a whine, or a whimper...perhaps even a child's cry...

Something urged him to go inside. Did he dare go in there?

He did dare. Striding over purposefully, he set the lamp down and gave the handle a heave...

When Eva saw Renard disappear through the door to the kitchens she grew bored. He was only going in to look for food. Besides, the house was rather drafty and she felt cold.

She took a wrong turn on her way back to the room and ended up in a different part of the house. A second living room, if you could believe it.

And then the cold steel of a knife pressed at her throat.

"Don't make a sound," whispered Amelie Mordant. "Or I will leave you here for him to find you."

Eva tried to push away, but the knife had teeth and it bit her. She felt a warm trickle of blood crawl down over her collarbone. Amelie chuckled into her ear. "I have a riddle for you," she whispered. "What is greater than God, more wicked than the devil, the poor have, the rich desire, and the starving cannot eat?"

"Nothin'," gasped Eva.

Amelie's other hand groped cruelly at Eva's body. She felt through the fabric of the nightdress and gave Eva's breasts a pinch. "Smart girl. Smart, smart girl."

"What you want from me?"

"Your life."

She shoved Eva forward. "You come with me and do exactly as I say."

Eva had no choice. Amelie led her deeper into the house, away from Renard. They stopped at the end of a lonely hallway. A wide bookcase stood at the dead end, seemingly out of place. No other furniture surrounded it. Amelie felt all over the shelf for something; a secret catch. She pulled it and it swung open to a small doorway.

The door led to a tiny, windowless room. Really more of a closet. A sleeping mat lay unrolled in the corner. Drafts of air blew in from old grates on the sides. Eva knew this could not be the servants' quarters. These were secret rooms.

"Papa told me about these," whispered Amelie wickedly. "He used to dally with Gaspard in here. Right under the Madame's nose."

The rooms stank of mold and paraffin from the lamp in the corner that threw a red wash all over the barren walls. Eva backed up into Amelie.

"I won't."

"Move forward, bitch. I'll cut your throat."

She did not want to go inside. But the knife bit deep,

and Amelie gave her a rough push forward.

Then she saw the child.

"My son," said Amelie, by way of explanation.

Eva had not heard much about little Henri. He was the legal son of Renard Mauricette and, in fact, a bastard. The child's hair was a very deep black with thick, shiny curls. He looked very much like Amelie. But unless the light of the room was deceiving, Eva saw his skin was not pale and white, but a very gentle brown.

A black child.

"You stay here," said Amelie in a low whisper. "And you make no sound. Or I cut off the air and leave you here to suffocate."

"With the child?" gasped Eva.

Amelie only laughed. She began to shut the door.

"No!" Eva screamed. But the door banged shut. And little Henri began to wail.

Amelie waited breathlessly outside the bookcase for some noise to stir within the house. She hoped that oaf Renard could not hear the muffled commotion going on in the secret room. But nothing moved, and all was still. The Mauricette house had been well-built; sound did not travel as well as the chilly air.

Resolving to her purpose, Amelie now inspected the bookcase. It was this bookcase the scrying spell had shown her in her dreams. Most of the stuff on there was junk reading, etiquette books and travel novels and a single, battered cookbook. A ledger book or two. But what better way to hide something than in plain sight?

In a trice she discovered what she had been looking for. It was stuffed between a farmer's almanac and an old copy of Aesop's Fables. Bound in simple brown leather, no title on the spine. Nothing to indicate it was anything more than an ordinary book...

But it was not. Holding it to her chest, every nerve in her body alight with anticipation, she slid through the halls of the Left Wing to a square of delicious moonlight. And reverently she opened it.

This book had been the property of Amelie Mordant's mother. It had been her diary, of a sorts, and also her grimoire.

Amelie flipped quickly through the spells. These were not the spells of healing and restoring. They had been passed down and performed by wicked women and men, and so they were spells to bind, destroy, and injure.

Written on the first page was a brief inscription from her mother. Amelie had little interest in this, but she read anyway. And it went as follows;

From the hand of Marie Alfonsine.

I am the child of a slave, and a creole. I was brought up to know the arts of magic and destruction so all may fear me and what I can do.

My mother's master was Robert Mordant, and his son, my half-brother, I have taken for a lover. For him I bore a daughter, Amelie, because his wife was barren. I then poisoned the wife so that I could have Louis to myself. Some may call me a wicked woman. But by the time this book is found, I will have long since passed into the second world beyond all the punishments of this one. So; I do not care. In wickedness the greatness of women truly lies. My daughter will grow up with her father's name but she will learn the secrets of my art, and become twice the conjurer I ever was.

I have taken many lovers but I know only one husband, who is the devil. And to him, and to you, daughter, I dedicate the secrets of this book.

-Mama

Amelie shut the book and smiled. The negress had been taken care of. The book had been acquired. And now, to find Renard.

As she crept on through the Mauricette house, as Eva LaLaurie pounded her fists on the stone wall that imprisoned her, Renard was emerging from the cellar. But he did not ascend up the same staircase he had climbed to enter it. He had discovered a short tunnel leading under the house's foundation to an unlocked trapdoor.

Near this trapdoor he found the skeleton. It was a small skeleton. It seemed to crumble when he held the light to it. He suspected it had been a woman; indeed, some scraps of an old-fashioned dress still clung to the bones. A slave woman, put there to rot in the cellar by one of his ancestors.

Renard would have been fine to leave her there to keep watch over the dark and lonely bowels of the house. But he thought of Eva. She believed bones must be laid to rest with respect. And knew he must bury the poor wretch come morning. For now, however, the poor dead woman must wait a little longer.

Continuing on, he opened the door to find himself in the Lower Gardens. A shower of leaves and loose dirt descended on his shoulders, but he crawled through and came upright in the center of the little pavilion. Over the years the servants had kept the pavilion trimmed and tailored to a certain kind of wildness. It reminded him, painfully, of Eva's cabin garden.

With that thought, he vowed to build her a house much like the one she had lost. A brick house with a bigger garden.

He emerged from the pavilion and made his way to the front door of the house. The night was cold, October-cold, but this was Louisiana, and even the cold was sweet. His little exploration had invigorated him. When he got inside he would crawl back in the immense feather bed next to Eva's supple body. He might turn her over and slide inside her, making love to her until dawn came.

He opened the front door easily. Renard never locked it. Why should he? He had nothing to fear. Rue Cher was his home. And Eva, naked and beautiful, was on his mind. Lost in impure thoughts, he never felt the presence of another until the barrel of the pistol pressed against his kidneys.

"Be still, Monsieur," purred Louis Mordant. "And make   no   sound."

CHAPTER EIGHT

Eva paced around the tiny apartments. The lamp had sputtered out. They were totally, absolutely, dark. But soon her eyes grew accustomed to the night. Henri had stopped crying; now he only looked at her expectantly. A little over a year old, he was too young to understand what was happening. He was only afraid. For a child that age, he spoke very little.

The two rooms were completely empty but for a wooden table. No windows; the only exit was through the bookcase, which could not be opened from the inside anyhow. Eva strained and heaved against it in vain while Henri watched.

"Don't suppose you got a crowbar in them nappies," she said to Henri. He stared back at her blankly.

Eva guessed that Amelie would try to murder Renard with her safely out of the way and leave her there to die with Henri. The thought was enough to keep trying for an escape.

But the room was only made of wood, after all, and even wood could be torn apart...

The boy moved himself to the corner and sat huddled with his arms around his knees. Eva looked again at the small vent along the bottom of the wall. She got on her hands and knees and crawled over to it.

"Help!" she screamed into the grate. Some draft of air snatched her voice away and strangled it.

The grate was about the size of an encyclopedia. Only Henri could fit through a thing like that, but then where did it lead? Was it a long drop to the basement or the cellar?

She wrapped her fingers around the bar and tugged. It did not budge.

"Oh, hell," she swore. She braced herself and pulled again. Eva was a strong woman, but the Mauricette builders had been talented, and the grate whined but still did not move.

Finally she gave up and sat down. Henri looked across the room at her with his lamp-like eyes. He crawled through the darkness and sat next to her.

"You cold?" she asked him. The little boy wore only a thin shirt, a sagging nappy and no shoes. He nodded but made no move to come closer.

"A fine pickle we're in," sighed Eva, and leaned her head back to think.

Her hand strayed to the pouch she wore around her neck; Sam's pouch. She opened it in the darkness and felt around. Superstition, Renard might have said. It's scientifically impossible...

It was Renard she thought of as she tied a little knot in one of the wiry hairs. A tear slid down her cheek. Sam, Renard, Nelson, Esau...wherever they were, she hoped they were alright.

Later, Eva's gaze fell on the shadowy form of the wooden table. It looked like strong wood- but could it splinter? Could it break?

A mile from where Eva sat in the secret rooms, Sam LaLaurie tossed in a fit of dreaming. Sam, unlike his siblings, had his own sleeping place in the cabin because he moved about so much and talked in his sleep. These days he dreamed a lot- mostly nightmares.

In his dreams that night Sam saw Nelson and Esau

being dragged up to a Poplar tree, kicking and yelling. He saw them drop from the end of a rawhide rope. And he saw the white men start the fire under their dangling feet. At this point in the dream that was now becoming familiar, he'd trained himself to look away. But he could still hear their screams.

Sam had the seer's ability, for his mismatched eye could often pierce into the second world, as his Nanny would have called it, where the spirits lived.

Doctors would say he had hallucinations, 'fits of the imagination'. Science had lots of explanations for his condition. But Sam knew what he saw.

Once the nightmare of Nelson and Esau was over, Sam again fell into a deep sleep. And then he dreamed of Eva.

He dreamed she was sitting in a cell all alone. A shaft of moonlight illuminated her face, which was drawn and sad.

"Help," she said, in the spirit-language that was not English or Creole, but something else, something with round vowels and short words. The ancestors' language. And she pointed.

His gaze turned and now he was somewhere else. He saw Renard Mauricette being dragged down near his fishing hole. Two white men, one fat and one skinny, had him bound. One of them had a club. The other had a gun.

He turned and looked at Eva. She mouthed the word again: "Help."

He shook his head. This was white folks' business. But Eva looked so sad and it nearly broke his heart. He woke up.

"Mama's gun," he said aloud, but it was not his voice coming out of his mouth.

The spirit world had given him a command.

A couple years ago his mother had taken up with a white man from over the river. A fellow named Crowley. A meaner bastard there never was, and he beat Sam's mother mercilessly. Luckily Crowley had drunk himself to death two years ago and he left nothing in the cabin but the smell of moonshine and a loaded revolver that he had once threatened to blow out Sam's eye with.

Sam knew where this gun was but he had never in his life took a shot with it. He didn't know if it even worked anymore. But he extracted it from the hiding place and crept over the creaky wood to the door. His heart pounded nightmarishly. If Momma woke up and found him she would skin him alive.

But he made it outside. And then the feeling came on him so strong, the feeling that some force had burrowed its way behind his heart and was pulling him, like a fish on a hook, to some unknown conclusion. He began to run towards the forest.

Louis Mordant led Renard off the property at gunpoint. He was not playing the gentleman tonight. He did not even allow Renard to return for his coat.

"What do you have to gain from this?" Renard demanded as they walked. "My quarrel is with Amelie, not you."

"Ah, but I have a quarrel with you," smiled Louis under his moustache. "Your mother and sister showed up this evening with lots of fine things to say about you. I figured I ought to chance my luck tonight, while they were gone."

"What do you want with me?"

"You are a meddling son of a bitch," said Louis. "And it's better to have you out of the way. My monetary interests in Rue Cher notwithstanding."

He chuckled. "And- you are still not technically

divorced from my daughter. I made sure of that."

"What?!"

"Indeed," said Mordant, enjoying himself immensely. "You would be surprised how far my money stretches, Renard. Anyone can be bribed. All rich men know this."

"I have the documents-"

"Forgeries," dismissed Louis. "Commissioned by me, to put you at ease. Easily recognized for what they are. No, no, my boy. You are still, legally, Amelie's husband, and the father of her child."

Renard turned on him incensed. "How dare-"

"Ah, ah," chortled Louis, jabbing the gun in his stomach. "You do have Gaspard's temper. But none of his charm, I'm afraid. Keep walking."

But Renard would not. They were hours yet from

dawn; anything could happen in the dark night that could be covered up come morning. He would not be marched to his own execution.

They stood at the bottom of Master's Hill. The charred scent of Rue Cher still hung in the air like ashes. Not a single light flickered; none were awake. Louis's frown deepened and for a frightening moment Renard thought he saw his father's own face.

"Move," snarled Louis.

"Whatever business you have with me we do it right here. Or you shoot me dead and be done with it."

Clearly the older man had not bargained for this rebellion. He scowled. "I forgot you were a damned soldier." Louis sucked his lower lip in and gave a low, piercing whistle.

A loping figure emerged from the line of trees: Charles St. Joseph. Of course. Wearing his usual clothes and holding a length of fraying rope. In the moonlight his waxy face looked even more monstrous.

"Trouble, sir?" grinned St.Joseph.

"Help me secure him," said Louis. Renard turned to move away; of course he was too slow. Charles' hand shot out and, using Renard's weight against him, slammed him to the ground. Then Charles landed a lead-foot kick in the knee of Renard's bad leg.

Renard gasped; light exploded behind his eyes. He tried to stumble to his feet, but they had him to the ground once more, Louis keeping pressure on the old wound in his leg. Charles tied Renard's hands efficiently behind his back in an iron knot.

"Wonderful," said Louis. He lifted Renard to his feet and they frog-marched him forward.

They headed down into Rue Cher but then turned off towards the woods, skirting the edge of destroyed houses. They passed the remains of Eva's cabin and then clumped on through the thicket. Renard had to be dragged part of the way. He had already picked up on their plan.

If only he had his leg healed! If only Eva had been able to make him some more of her medicine...

"So it's to be a lynching, then? Decided not to get your friends in the hoods out for this one, did you?"

"Talk all you want, boy," said Louis gruffly. They moved deeper into the woods, Charles leading the way. Louis could hardly see in the dark and kept stumbling along with Renard. Renard insulted them as loud as he could without shouting. He was trying to work the ropes off his wrist.

St.Joseph had tied him well. Long experience with these unsavory kinds of things, no doubt.

But anything could be untied, and Renard's hands were flexible and deft; a painter's, with a soldier's training. He ran his fingers along the edges of the knot and got a mental picture of its type. He almost laughed.

St. Joseph had been a farmer's son, and the knots he knew were of that kind. And the rawhide itself was old. The man's mistake had been not wetting and braiding the rope before he tied it. Renard began to work at the knot-puzzle with his thumbnail.

They arrived at a spot near the river: the fishing-hole, where Renard knew some black men from Rue Cher liked to frequent. Here the moon made lace through the treetops, washing everything in a beautiful blue light. The three mens' skins were white, but all other colors showed up in deepest black. They leaned the young Mauricette against a tree.

Charles lit a cigarette. "This is it," he told Louis. "They like to come here to fish."

"You're sure?"

"I know them better than they know themselves,"

snorted Charles. "Beasts of habit."

Renard caught on to their plan. "So you want to pin the blame on the negroes for this. Set it up to look like they lynched me. Rally up common sentiment to drive them out. If the whites weren't sympathetic to your cause, they will be now. Am I correct?"

"Absolutely," said Louis. He chuckled. "You are your father's son, Renard. But with none of his imagination- or, as I said, his charm. We're going torture you first."

"It wouldn't suffice to just hang me, I suppose," said Renard.

"Only reason I agreed to this," said Charles with a nasty grin. "I imagine the gentle ladies of our society will be quite squeamish to see what's become of the handsome Mauricette brat."

Louis straightened his overcoat and stood back. As an aesthete he had to appreciate the morbid beauty of the scene. Renard Mauricette looked very much like a younger version of his father. Tall, well-formed, comfortably arrogant. He leaned his back against a tree to support his throbbing leg. His slanted cat's eyes appraised them. Still thinking he could talk his way out of this one, no doubt.

Unfortunately Charles St. Joseph had none of Louis's appreciation. He was merely a sadist. He found the rope he'd hidden and moved towards the captive. Charles has never liked those cowardly Big Whites, with all their talk and money. He was anticipating teaching the young Mauricette a painful lesson.

"A fine one you chose," Renard said to Louis, jutting his chin at the henchman. "I expect if he ever had an idea it would die of loneliness."

"Quiet," growled Charles. In his excitement the rope had got itself tangled. He fumbled with it clumsily.

"And built like a brick shithouse," Renard went on. "You blame the negroes for this country going to the dogs? Look at this piece of work right here- there's your dead weight, Mordant. An ape in a man's clothing."

Snarling, Charles dropped the rope.

"My God. If he moved any slower he'd be going backwards."

Renard grunted as the other man socked him one on the jaw. A bruise flowered across his face like a black lily.

"That's right." Louis waved the gun in Renard's face. "Be quiet."

"We ought to just shoot him," said Charles. He had finally got the rope unknotted. Renard tensed.

What happened next seemed to turn the world on its head. A sudden bang echoed nearby. All three men jumped; the forest seemed to skitter into life.

"Gunshot?" said Charles.

"One moment," said Louis, swiveling the gun.

There was another, weaker sound. And a howl that could have only come from a human.

"What the devil-" said Louis Mordant.

Amelie returned for the boy an hour later. She had intended to leave him there with Eva LaLaurie. She could have framed the woman for Henri's kidnapping and attributed it to their sudden disappearances. But in the end Amelie needed Henri. A living child was more useful than a dead one. All witches knew that.

Amelie expected the negro woman to be demure and pacified when she opened the secret door. She held the knife out in front of her just in case.

Henri was sitting in the middle of the room with his

hands over his ears.

"Get up," she said, striding over to him. "And where's that bitch?"

"Right here," said Eva, and leapt at her from the side.

The beam of shattered wood caught Amelie a glancing blow in the back of the head. Eva stepped behind the woman and hit her again in the center of her back. The beam broke along a splinter and Amelie shrieked. The knife dropped from her hands.

Eva kicked it away and the dance began. The rotten old bitch was stronger than she looked. She launched herself at Eva's ankles and brought her tumbling down to level with her.

Eva got a good fistful of Amelie's hair and pulled with all her strength. Her neck jerked back; she howled; Eva roared. Those hands that had healed and tended were now clenched and ready to kill. She knew she would have to bring the other woman to her knees. There would be no mercy here.

"Mama!" sobbed little Henri.

"I'll kill you," sobbed Amelie. Her scalp burned like a firebrand. Eva still had a grip on her hair and was twisting her neck back and forth. She raked Eva's legs with her nails, tried to bite her, hit her...

But Eva had spent long days wrestling with her cousins in the dirt. Amelie's experience with violence had been beating servants who couldn't hit back.

"I'll kill you!" shrieked the woman.

"Try it!"

Amelie dug her nails viciously into Eva's flesh. But the healer was used to pain, she had a good ten pounds on the other woman, and her temper had focused on a morbid intent. In a battle of fists the advantage was hers. She landed Amelie Mordant another blow that sent her crumpling to the floor again. Eva staggered to her feet. She charged the other woman.

Amelie reared! A splinter of the broken beam, about the length of a man's hand, buried itself in the muscle of Eva's thigh. Eva hardly felt it. Grabbing Amelie's wrist to fend off further assault, her other hand seized the rope of oily black hair again. She pivoted on one foot and hurled the struggling Amelie away from her. The creole woman's head met the floor with a sickening crack.

A terrified Henri fled through the ajar door and vanished. Amelie struggled to get up. Then she changed her mind and began struggling for the knife. The blows to her head and temple had addled her wits; she had misjudged Eva's strength and ruthlessness. For Eva used the moment to kick Amelie in the ribs and stagger through the open door in Henri's wake. A trail of blood followed her.

Amelie realized her mistake too late. She held the knife, but not the weapon.

"No!" she shrieked. "No! No!"

Laughing like a madwoman, Eva slammed the bookcase shut.

♘

He had seen the men cart off the Mauricette into the woods. They hadn't seen him watching from the shadows. Little Sam had fired the gun once, but with its age it would not fire again.

And anyway, Sam was reluctant to do any more than lure them away. He certainly wasn't about to go after them with some busted old gun. But he sure had got their attention. They were looking around wildly for the source of the noise. He deepened his voice and bellowed in his best white-man-voice imitation,

"Now what's going on here, fellows?"

If he hadn't been scared out of his wits their reaction

might have been funny.

"Who's there?" shouted the squat, ugly one with the rope.

"I demand you put that poor bastard down!" Sam boomed shakily. He took several paces back; the hulking man started for the trees.

Renard took the opportunity to give his wrists a solid wrench. The frayed rawhide snapped. Louis was distracted and spooked, deciding whether he should stay and just shoot Renard or make a run for it. He took a moment too long and slipped his guard. Renard slipped the last of the knots off his wrist and felled the man with a blow to the side of the head.

Then he was running, running in the opposite direction. His leg was in agony, but an agony that could wait. The blasts of Mordant's pistol shredded bark from the trees, but in seconds Renard had escaped the circle of moonlight and the range of the gun. He could hear St. Joseph crashing around trying to find the source of the strange voice, which seemed to come from everywhere at once, and was muddled by the screams of Louis.

Renard didn't know how, and he didn't know why, but he was certain that voice belonged to none other than Sam LaLaurie.

He did the first thing that came to his head: he began to whoop, a demonic cry that carried far and wide across the forest. Hoping to lure the man away from Sam, who was doing the same. Meanwhile Louis, roaring like a wild boar, came crashing through the woods after him, firing at whatever moved.

The forest didn't suffocate; any sound they made carried and echoed through the trees. Still shouting nonsense, Renard and Sam seemed to orient themselves in the same direction. They were leading the two men towards the village.

The wind soon took the noise to the inhabitants of Rue Cher. And once the stray hounds started baying, soon every soul was up and lighting candles.

Certain that the Klan had returned, or at the very least some demon had descended, the bravest evacuated the houses in droves, and the rest buried themselves under blankets and prayed it would be over. At that moment the moon burst through a knot of cloud and shone her brilliance on the tree line. Those who lived on the edge of Rue Cher were treated to the startling sight of little Sam LaLaurie running like the very hounds of hell, shrieking his head off and waving a gun he'd got from God-knows-where.

Not far behind Sam was a balding white man that would have been an all-too-familiar face to the people of Rue Cher. In another life he might have caught up with the boy. But not in this one. Sam sprinted for the Low Rivers, a knot of cabins owned by the poorest of Rue Cher, the white man in hot pursuit. Then he seemed to vanish.

By then Renard had split into another direction. Louis Mordant knew he could not let the Maurciette make it back to civilization to tell the tale of what had happened. But Mordant could not afford to be seen, either. In his panicked rage, and unused to the adrenaline of combat, he had fired the gun one too many times. A single bullet remained.

But his pursuit did not last long. He stopped running. He had to. His breath was bursting out of him in wheezes. He shrank against a tree, spitting, heaving each breath like a scored pig. His vision swam before him. Such was the price one paid for luxury! A body that had been spoiled by appetite and comfort, and now threatened to fall to pieces at the slightest exertion. He had been confident- too confident.

And then there was Renard. Renard had forgotten the hole in his leg. It seemed to no longer exist. He felt no pain; he felt alive. He stopped and caught his breath. Then, driven by some unknown urge, he doubled back and followed the sounds of Louis's agitated grunting.

Renard did not have to go far. The older man had

collapsed to his hands and knees. A hand clutched his chest, wrenching at the fabric of his overcoat.

Louis Mordant looked up at the sound of footsteps. He hoped it was merely a deer, but he knew it was not. Every breath seemed to wrench a piece of his lungs out with it.

And then he saw the form of Gaspard Mauricette emerging from the tunnel of trees. Gaspard. His face blanched by moonlight and the distantly-rising sun. Louis gasped.

It was Gaspard as he had been- a young man. Laughing, arrogant, dangerous. Arrestingly handsome. Gaspard, come for his revenge... Louis blinked and cleared his vision. No, it was not Gaspard.

He raised the gun. His hands trembled violently.

"You are out of bullets, Monsieur, " said Renard Mauricette. And he stepped closer, perhaps to help the other to his feet.

But Renard had been mistaken. Louis squeezed the trigger and the Mauricette fell to his knees in a shower of leaves.

"Oh," said the younger man. But Louis hardly heard him. His heart, his heart, throbbed like an Indian drum but pierced through his skin like an arrow. There seemed to be two people emerging from the trees. No, not people. Shadows. Now three, now seven. Louis Mordant was seeing ghosts.

Gaspard, his dead wife, his dead concubine, the negress mother of Amelie, and an Indian, and a Negro, and countless more. In fact Louis was hallucinating. But shall we say he wasn't?

"Ah!" he gasped.

It was the sight of these creatures of the forest that would be his ultimate end. His old heart gave up the fight. Some folk believed that the soul fled the body and went to live in the second world. Others would say he had ridden the fastest chariot to hell.

In any case, Louis Mordant was dead.

Renard hauled himself out of the forest like a drowning man launching himself to the shore.
And he lay, bleeding. His leg was dead. And if he did not get something done about the bullet in his shoulder, he would surely bleed to death.

Call it luck, or fortune, or some mysterious magic of Sam LaLaurie's grandmother, in the form of a hair in a pouch around Eva LaLaurie's neck, Sam came eventually to the side of Renard Mauricette. Dawn was streaking the sky. A rosy dawn, like the kind that had graced the sky the morning Renard had painted Eva on his couch.

Sam was not carrying the gun anymore. In the few

months since he'd met Renard he had grown taller. They were almost of a height. Sam knelt in front of the Mauricette.

"You dyin'?" he said.

"I don't know," said Renard. "I'm not a doctor."

"I ought to leave you here," said Sam. "For what you done to Eva."

A new angle of attack. He lifted his eyebrows tiredly. "What did I do to Eva?"

"You brought that curse on her. You brought that curse into the village."

"What curse?"

Sam put his fingers to the bullet wound. He might have tended to it himself. Renard hissed. The boy's face was strangely hard and unforgiving. His mismatched eyes were narrowed.

"Somebody put a curse on you. I saw it when you came to get your leg fixed that first time. Told Eva you was no good but she wouldn't listen." He shook his head.

A curse indeed. Amelie's curse.

"I put the dolls on her door to break y'all apart. I knew what she was feelin' about you from the moment you left. But it didn't work. You just had to keep comin' after her! It was no good. And now look. She gonna be gone, the whole village gonna be gone. I can't- I can't go to her house no more, or sit on her step and tell her stuff-" young Sam broke off into sobbing.

"You think...you think I was to blame?"

"I know it," wept Sam. "And now what am I gonna do? She was s'posed to teach me. I wanted to be a doctor..."

"Get Eva," said Renard. "Or I'm going to die."

"Where is she?" said Sam, wiping his face.

"The big house."

"I'm not goin' there."

"You must, or I'll die."

"I don't care!" Sam shrieked. And he got up and ran away.

Renard rolled his eyes to the sky. He forgot what happened next. Perhaps he passed out.

Some folks from the village found him eventually. They recognized him, and they didn't like him, but they took him in anyway. He was carried into somebody's house. A dirty, scratchy place that indicated nothing about the character of its inhabitants other than their poverty. A woman bent over him.

"Eva?" he grunted.

"Naw I ain't no Eva," the woman snapped. "Now hush."

There were two men and two women. The men looked on disgustedly as the women tended to him.

"This is gonna hurt," one woman said. She was molding a paste of something in her hands. Shaping it into a wet green-brown ball.

"I don't care," said Renard. And then he added in case they weren't sure: "I don't want to die."

They ignored him.

"You sure that's how she did it?" asked another woman, to the one holding the ball.

"Yeah I'm sure, Sarie. I saw her do it myself."

They were talking about Eva.

The woman cut away the shirt from Renard's shoulder. She plucked the fibers being sucked into the wound. He had stopped bleeding.

A black-and-white cat found its way inside the cabin. Renard did not recognize it at first. It jumped up on the table and curled next to his leg. Patches of fur were gone. When it licked his sore wrist, he remembered.

"Hello, Boots," whispered Renard.

"Git!" shooed Sarie. But the cat didn't move.

"Leave it be. Are you taking the bullet out?"

"Ain't I tell you be quiet, white man?" she barked. But the hand putting the paste on his shoulder was gentle. "And no. It went clean through. Lucky for you. If it had bust that vein, you would be stone dead."

She tied up the wound with an old cloth.

"The herb slows the bleeding," she explained. "Eva taught me that."

The other woman, meanwhile, was heating an herb in some boiling butter over the fireplace. Renard recognized the smell; it was the same herb Eva had made into a tea for him the first time he'd gone to see her. Sure enough, a few minutes later the woman strained the fat and poured it into a cup of tea for him. "Drink."

He drank.

"Y'all too damn soft-hearted," said one of the men. "Should have just left him there. One less white man to go hurtin' someone else."

"You hush," snapped Sarie Jules. She turned back to Renard. "You ought to sleep."

"Yes Ma'am." He laid his spinning head back and let the herb carry him off to a murky kind of waking.

Eva appeared two hours later. The villagers were stunned to see her. She wore a nightdress and nothing on her head or feet, though it was cold and almost raining. Down one side of the nightdress was soaked with rusty bloodstains. Her eyes were sunken in her face.

Next to her walked Sam, who was carrying a small child on his shoulders. He led Eva to Sarie's house. They went inside.

At her appearance everyone stopped talking. Eva nodded a greeting. Sam put the child down on the porch and suffered to play with him. The boy looked frightened out of his mind. He ran from Sam and hid.

Inside the cabin Renard was sitting up and awake. He nearly didn't recognize Eva when she came through the wooden door. Hazy from the herb-tea, which Sarie had made viciously strong, he struggled to sit up and clear his vision.

"What happened to you?"

She shook her head. "I might ask you the same damn question."

The bullet had pierced his shoulder all the way through. Lucky, that. Eva hadn't the time nor energy nor equipment to be digging bullets out of people. She pulled Sarie's plaster off and washed the wound with whatever herbs were available and some strong moonshine. Renard went white but made no sound.

"Hmmph," said the men who watched him. "That's a tough bastard."

Eva glared at Renard when they said this. "You'll live," she pronounced icily.

"You're angry with me," he said, astonished. After what he had been through, she had no right to be.

"Oh, Renard." was all she replied, shaking her head.

 He shut his eyes and rested his head back. Let her be angry, then. He didn't care.

Then she sat down and asked Sarie if she had any yarrow powder. The woman brought it at once. Eva peeled up the bottom of her nightdress- the men blushed and looked away, except Renard- to reveal the vicious-looking hole. Calmly, Eva borrowed Sarie's tweezers and began to pull tiny wooden fragments from it. She washed it up herself and Sarie gave her more herbs and helped roll up the plaster with some water from the pump.

The awkward silence in the cabin was deafening. The two men grew bored, then uncomfortable, then left. Only Sarie and her friend remained.

"Y'know, Eva," said Sarie, "You taught us most everythin' we know about the healing and the herbs. I can fix stuff up pretty good now for myself."

Eva rested her head back in the chair and closed her eyes, mirroring Renard. "Good," she said. "It better come in handy when y'all move up North."

"You heard about it?" asked Sarie. "We was gonna break it you tomorrow..."

"I figured," said Eva. "Folks don't want to stay no place where the white folks can come round and burn and hang 'em anytime they please. Ain't no shame in movin' on, Sarie. I ain't mad for it."

"Since Esau died...and Nelson..."

Renard looked up. The herbal drug warped everything in front of him. But Eva's face swam out, clear as a picture...as a painting. He would have painted it then and called it *tranquility*. But then a single tear rolled out of her closed eyes, followed by another. Not tranquility, but grief.

"I don't wanna talk about Nelson, Sarie."

"Alright. Well, I was just lettin' you know. Folks is just gettin' their wits together. We gonna sell what we can and start up for the North."

"It's your decision."

"It's a shame," said Sarie Jules, who like Tom Shanter had never been able to hold her tongue, "that it had to turn out this way. Folks thought it might have been different. For you. For all of us."

"Different." Eva could not miss the implication. "Different for me how?"

"We just thought you would stick with your own folks, is all."

"Y'all got it all wrong," said Eva. And she turned to look at Renard. He was half-asleep, his slanted eyes staring back at her through a film of pain. A curious thought struck her; he had never looked more handsome. He looked like he had the first day he had come through her door and sat in her chair and asked her to fix his leg.

"It don't matter, anyhow," said Eva, "what's done is done."

"Maybe it do matter," said Sarie quietly. "Maybe you the one that was wrong."

"Good," sighed Eva. Another tear. It danced on the point of her chin, and fell. "Y'all go on and believe that."

They judged her because she had taken this man- this strange white man- when she should have been happy with one of their own. They saw it as a rejection, and they saw that rejection as the beginning of every problem that had followed. But they could never reject her. She was Eva, she was their healer. No matter what she did, Eva was a part of their community as much as the river and the forest and the swamp. No matter where they went on in the world, she would still be a part of them. So Sarie spoke with judgment and disapproval, but not with hatred.

♘

They left little Henri with Sam's family. Renard insisted Eva come with him back to the Mauricette house, and she did.

Eva decided to let Renard handle Amelie. But when he entered the secret room, the grate was missing and Amelie was gone. They found her mother's grimoire on the floor, shredded to pieces. To them it appeared to be no more than an old journal. Curiouser and curiouser, because every tattered page was perfectly blank .

The body of Louis Mordant disappeared from where it had fallen. The next day a fisherman trawling in the river pulled it up, crab-eaten and bloated and soiled.

They never found Charles St. Joseph. To find out what happen to him you had to ask Sam. He would have said to ask the people in Low Rivers. And they would have said, why don't you ask the 'gators ?

In the end Renard made the sale on the Rue Cher property. He wrote a letter to his mother and sister from their seat at the Mauricette summer home to inform them they would not be returning to the main house, and their things would be delivered to them at the summer home post haste. They would receive a yearly sum of two thousand dollars, collected from the rented properties in West Rue Cher. Enough to live on with little left for luxury.

His mother and sister did not write back.

Later in the year, one morning, the remaining residents of Rue Cher were hand-delivered notes for one hundred dollars, a sum to go to each household. The families could cash these notes as soon as they reached the North.

The story spread and made the local papers. But Renard Mauricette could not be reached for comment.

He had disappeared, and was never seen in Rue Cher again.

EPILOGUE I

In Boston they called her many names, and 'doctor' was seldom one of them, though a doctor indeed she was. In the high society of New England there would be no allowances for women of her stature, no matter how much education she had attained. Prejudice ran deeper than sense. That, like the stink coming off the old Charles River, was a fact of life she'd never grow used to.

Now Eva LaLaurie, now four years removed from her humble country life in the Louisiana backwoods, sat at her writing desk and read the letter over. It had been written in a slanting, childish scrawl. But the language was formal.

It was from Sam, dated a few months prior. His mother was now in Chicago with the rest of the family. The woman had sent for him these last few months. Sam was working at a factory. Too old for school, Sam needed to support his brothers and sisters and earn a wage.

He added, in a postscript, that he missed her endlessly.

Eva set the letter down. She had read it a hundred times over, reconstructing the face of her young cousin in her mind as he had been three years ago, when last she had seen him.

Sam, like her old life in Rue Cher, was a dream and a ghost of her past. All their hopes and dreams then had seemed so trivial. In a single night they had vanished into smoke. And now her dreams were different. She was a different person. And so was Sam.

She then went to her armoire. She put on pearl earrings, matching necklace, and moved to the wardrobe. The outfit she selected was in good but not extravagant taste. Her makeup was light; and also tasteful. The pearls glowed against her dark skin. A different woman stared at her from the mirror. A woman of steel.

The child Henri Christoff looked up from his picture book to watch her. It was hard not to feel, in his childish mind, that 'Auntie Eva' was not preparing to leave him behind every time she put on new clothes. The boy did not like to be alone.

"W-w-w-w-here are y-you going?" he asked.

"Uncle and I are attending a party."

"C-c-can I c-c-ome?"

A delicate, sweet, wisp of a child. Henri Christoff would never grow very big. What he lacked in size he earned in heart. Eva went over and kissed him.

"No darlin'. But I'll bring you somethin' when I'm back. And Marie can read you a lil' piece for bed."

She could not lose her country drawl any more than the boy could lose his stammer. Just as well.

Before Eva left she had a word with Marie about bedtime, and then she swept down the stairs and out to the street and the cold. A tall figure waited on the curb. He had been warming up the car, and now prepared to open the door for her.

At the sight of Renard, Eva's anxieties dissipated. In Boston he kept his hair short, which brought out the sharp angles of his features with even more intensity. He had also returned to the tailored suits and sharp patent shoes. He looked recklessly handsome as ever, and he grinned when he saw her.

"Well, Miss Eva."

"Well, Renard."

He kissed her in the street and let her in the car, and then they were off to a slow crawl down the streets. It had taken Eva a while to get used to automobiles. Now, she didn't mind so much.

"I thought we'd do something different tonight," he said.

"What you mean? We aren't going to Stacy's?"

Stacy Bueller was an heiress friend- a tolerant woman, a writer. She often hosted dinner parties for Boston elites who didn't ascribe to 'traditional' ways of thinking. Eva did not really enjoy these parties, but it was good to make friends with the people there. They liked her, for all her country ways.

"Afraid not," said Renard. "You'll never believe why."

"Why?"

He turned down an unfamiliar street. A vein worked in his jaw. "Amelie is back. Amelie is at Stacy's."

"Amelie...Amelie Mordant? Henri's-"

"The very same," said Renard. He took another turn. They were heading towards the train station. Eva did not question this; Renard would have his moments of impulse. Perhaps in place of their evening at Stacy Bueller's he had planned something else.

"I ran into her leaving Stacy's, on my way to get you. She's taken up with some oil tycoon. I swear- that woman's got spies all over the country. It can't be coincidence for her to turn up here."

He paused. "She asked about Henri."

"Our Henri?"

"Yes, Eva."

Eva's heart clenched. "She can't have him," she

343

declared firmly.

"She doesn't want him," Renard assured her. His hand grasped for hers; finding it, he brought it to his lips. Then his mouth found the ruby ring on her wedding finger, and he kissed that too. A ring of engagement. Eva and Renard were not yet married.

"Why are we going to the station, Renard?" Eva asked. He flicked her a look but didn't reply.

They pulled in to South Station just in time for the arrival of the Eastbound Train. Renard limped over to her side and let her out. Eva heard its slow churning noise long before she saw it. Renard put his arm round her shoulders, which earned them more than a few glances.

"We waitin' for somebody?" asked Eva, to hide her unease. Renard seemed bent on these kind of displays of affection. More than once some catcalls had turned into heated arguments. And even, once, a fight. Eva had to repeat the question.

"Yes," he allowed.

"Who?"

"Damn it, woman. Allow yourself the surprise."

A tall figure came walking up the rows, carrying a very tattered brown bag. A boy. Renard, grinning, pointed with his chin. Eva squinted behind her spectacles. Her eyesight had never been perfect, but with Renard's patronage and the help of a kindly eye doctor, things were much improved. Through the miasmic haze of the station the figure slowly became familiar.

Eva shrieked, "Sam!"

Then they were running towards each other, propriety forgotten, and she was swinging around in his big-big arms that could now lift her all the way off her feet. Her little cousin had grown. Yet he still had the mismatched eyes, and the cajun drawl, and he smelled the same, and felt the same. Eva hugged him and didn't want to let go. Renard limped over to join the fray.

Sam's arrival had startled them out of familiar patterns. It appeared Renard had intended the boy to stay on. Ever since they had first received the letter from Eva's relatives out in Chicago, Renard had established regular contact and insisted on the boy coming to Boston.

"There are more opportunities in the Northeast," he had written, "And Sam will be able to go to a proper school."

His mother had refused, and hid Renard's letter. But Sam rooted it out and wrote back a letter of his own: he was going.

So now their apartments had become quite crowded. Eva had months to go before obtaining her license. Sam slept in the painting room and made such a small impression that they hardly noticed his presence. And little Henri idolized the smooth-talking Sam.

Still, Renard's apartments were in a white neighborhood. The locals had suffered Eva's presence, but Sam's appearance became too much. All of Renard's money, which flowed as loosely as his tongue, could not overcome that prejudice.

Things reached a boiling point when Sam was confronted by a gang of white teenagers a block from the house and beaten senseless.

Then Eva began to talk of leaving.

"All my affairs are in Boston," protested Renard. "I can't leave."

"It's dangerous, Renard, us bein' here."

"Then we will move."

"Where?"

"Another block."

"With different white folks, you mean? They gonna dig us out as long as they see me with you. We got to go somewhere more tolerant. That's what you said, when we came up here. You said it would be more 'tolerant'. Look, I'm afraid to walk out my damn door."

Renard had to concede. But in the end the thing that truly spurred him to a decision was that Amelie had discovered their whereabouts. She showed up one morning in an automobile and waited on the curb, smoking, until someone took notice.

Renard went down to speak with her.

"Why are you here?"

She had sunken in the face. Much of her former beauty had leaked out of her. She looked lined and tired. The luxurious black hair, now cut brutally short under the chin in the fashion, looked limp. Her father's death had drained her. But the green eyes still bore the familiar hatred and malice.

"For Henri. Allow me to see my son."

Renard went inside and fetched the little boy. But he was frightened of his mother. He hid behind Renard's leg.

"Say hello, Henri," said Renard.

"H-h-h-h-" the boy could hardly get a word out. "H-h-hello."

"He stammers?" snapped Amelie. "An unpleasant habit. You should get rid of it, Renard."

"The boy or the stammer? And he's a fine boy. Do you know the father?"

349

Amelie tittered at this. "What do you think?"

"I think not."

"Quite right." She tossed her cigarette. "Things are not well back in Rue Cher."

"I have heard."

"Your mother and sister are married."

"Wonderful. I was tiring of their letters anyway. I can save their yearly allowance for myself."

She looked at him. This was a different Amelie. And a different Renard.

"Father was sunk in debt," she said. "I did not know. That's why he was bent on getting that negro land."

"A pity," said Renard, without pity.

"He was murdered." Her eyes flashed. "I still believe you had a hand in it."

Renard had done everything in his power to block out the memories of that night. He remembered watching the big Mordant die.

"I don't know what you're talking about. Did you come the three hundred miles to ask me that? I could have written and saved you the expense."

"No. I am in Boston for business."

"Honest, business, I hope. Still playing with your books and potions?" His voice was barbed. He was not ready to forgive her. She did not deserve to be forgiven.

The Amelie of the past would have risen to his bait and met him word for word. But this Amelie only lit another cigarette. Her teeth were yellower than he remembered.

"You can have your jokes," she said. "I did not come here to apologize."

"Neither did I."

She looked at him under heavy-lidded eyes. She sucked down the smoke deeply and blew it in his face. "Take care of the boy," she said. "For all he's a damn negro. A damn mistake."

She wanted to hurt him, but couldn't find and opening. So she had settled for shock at the boy's expense. Renard held Henri's shoulders protectively and said, "I will. He deserves a good mother."

Amelie slouched into her car. Renard had a hundred more words on his tongue ready to unleash at her. His memory was long and his heart was hard. But even this victory tasted bitter in his mouth. She left, and he stayed silent.

He looked about at the empty street. The neighborhood was fiercely clean. Done up in all that wonderful New England austerity. The houses were extravagant. The air was cold and unfriendly.

A memory swam to his head: sitting on Eva's porch, watching the garden overflow with flowers, the buzz of hummingbirds, the purring of a black-and-white cat...Country comforts. He missed the Louisiana heat. He missed what might have been.

He turned and went inside.

Renard had a cousin in the French Colonies. He wrote to this cousin in December. They received a response in March.

By then Eva's school was completed. Sam had apprenticed at a carpenter's and was making furniture. Henri showed little interest in anything but his books. Life went on, but something had changed. A kind of restlessness settled among them.

"Renard," said Eva one night, as they lay in bed, "What you know 'bout the Caribbean?"

"It's hot as the devil's throne," he said. She giggled. "No, I mean it."

"Me too. I've been there- once, a very long time ago, with Father. It was...strange."

"Strange how?" she sat up on her elbows, suddenly eager. "There's another colored gal at the college. Her Papa was from Trinidad. Mama was white."

"Oh?"

"I was just wonderin', you know, if things might be different there." She fiddled with his hair and flicked her eyes to his. "For us, I mean."

She was getting at something. Renard frowned. "You mean, if they live more out in the open there?"

She nodded. "Yes. You know- it was just a thought I had. I thought we should go, sometime. Before I start my practice."

His first instinct, to reject the idea, must have showed on his face. For Eva became more determined.

"Fact is, Renard, what we doin' here ain't- isn't- really livin'. It's hidin'. You got to hide me from your business partners. You got to hide Henri. And now Sam gotta hide too. You hole up in here with me but we can't go out regular. It's just like Rue Cher."

Something accusatory lurked under her tone, and Renard found himself getting defensive. Back and forth they argued. He couldn't just leave his businesses in Boston to take care of themselves. Did she think money grew on trees? Hadn't he promised her they would find a way to be together- openly together? Well, he was just waiting, that was all. She should be more patient.

But Eva countered with a vigor he had not expected.

And Renard found himself losing ground. She didn't care about his businesses. You could do business from anywhere in the world these days. And what about her feelings? She was grateful for him putting her through doctor school, but that didn't mean she should be bound somewhere she didn't like. And what about Henri?

White society would have nothing to do with them. Black society- and who could indeed blame them- was extremely insular and defensive. They liked Eva's choice of mate even less than the people of Rue Cher had. Everywhere they turned the young couple found themselves confronted with the problem of their race- a problem that didn't matter at all in their inner lives, even as it dictated everything about their outward ones.

When Renard agreed that point, Eva pressed home. They would just go on a little vacation. They would just see. She got her hands on a picture book and pointed out different places they might visit. Martinique was selected. They knew enough passing

French to operate there.

Renard then wrote to his cousin, sidestepping Eva's background, and the trip was arranged.

"You didn't tell him?" Eva demanded, reading over the cousin's response, which was full of my dears and upon my words.

"We aren't staying with him anyhow," countered Renard. "Let him figure out his prejudice when we meet. He is for the convenience."

Before they left Boston, Renard paid a visit to the jeweler's and made a choice selection.

And in early May, the little family found themselves pushing off from shore aboard a Baltimore steamship, heading for a New World.

EPILOGUE II

The smell of frangipani hung on the air. Here, summer did not come on the heels of a wet, squelching cold. Here, summer stretched, far into the distance, like a beautiful dream from which there was no waking.

The mornings burst open. The nights descended. A quiet and a peace like no other; a stillness that broke only at the sounds of nature's mysteries.

Was she home?

She rolled in the great bed and saw the flash of curly black hair. Two eyes appeared under it, fluttering to life. And then, a smile.

He pulled her under him. His body was heavy with exhaustion from the night before, but they were awake now, and the soft light coming in through the slatted windows made them both appear younger and more beautiful.

"Good morning, wife," he murmured.

"Good mornin', husband," she replied.

He kissed her. She tasted very sweet.

"Are you happy?" he asked.

She didn't have to think. "Yes. I'm happy."

"Good."

Lying indolent within the sheets and the filmy
mosquito net, her loveliness had never appeared more
pronounced. He kissed her again. His hand groped at
a heavy breast.

"Oh- Renard. We can't. I'll be late-"

"Everyone here is late."

She giggled, and tried to look serious. "The doctor must be on time. She must set an example."

"Indeed. I suppose they taught you that at Boston University School of Medicine."

"They sure did. Now get up off me!"

Instead he buried his face in her neck and tickled her. Eva dissolved. She could never handle him when he did that.

But then he turned his head and kissed her again, and she gave in. As always. His lips teased against hers, and then his head dropped and he was suckling on her nipples.

"Renard-"

"Yes?"

"Don't stop..."

His kisses delved lower. And lower still. No removing of clothing was necessary; in this heat they slept perfectly naked. Renard parted her thighs with his strong hands and found the blossom therein. His tongue snaked out and Eva's moans pitched higher. Then he was plying her with two fingers, and now three...he had to hold her down. She shook under his kisses, his sucks, licks, gentlest bites at the soft skin of her thigh...

A storm of heat had gathered in Eva's belly. Her hands fisted in Renard's hair, now grown long and needing cutting. He made love to her like so; at once gentle, at once fierce. Love and war, fire and water. Her toes curled. He attended to her more fiercely, and it was her wetness she saw on his lips and beard when he rose up, his cock at full attention.

He took her hand and placed it on the length of him. Before this action might have shocked her, but Eva knew what she wanted and there were no mysteries about what would come next. She returned the favor...her lips wrapped around the head, and she took him to the base and the back of her throat made love to him in a few short strokes. They had practiced this way- she had grown to like it...

But Renard wanted the pleasure to be hers. He withdrew from the sweet wetness of her mouth. He turned her over on her stomach then and entered her from behind. In a smooth stroke all other thoughts were banished from Eva's mind.

"We don't stop," he murmured in her ear, "Until I feel you shake from it."

The little death he called it, and Eva knew why. And he went back on his heels and took her with him. He had speared her there, his cock feeling impossibly large and herself impossibly tight, and he thrust into her with slow, languid strokes, from the tip to the base, hard and intense; torturous.

If Eva had any more breath left in her it deserted her now. Renard's hand wrapped around her throat and raised her up, still impaled on him, her ear next to his mouth.

"You want this, Eva? More of this?"

"Yes," she gasped. He had started a new rhythm. His cock was teasing a sensitive spot deep inside her, and his hips worked against hers...

"No work today?" he chuckled. And he kissed her.

This was love. Bent over before him, even at his mercy Eva felt the bond between them. Stronger than steel. And he felt it too, for suddenly he felt to look on her face, and he turned her over and raised her legs on his shoulders. She accepted him. All of him, every long hot inch of him. This time he didn't hold back.

He gave it to her fully. He stroked her mercilessly until the cream ran out of her pussy and slicked against his thighs. Eva's soft, full-figure had never looked better. Under him like this, bared to him...he wanted to bite her, kiss her, love her, fuck her into sweet oblivion. And she wanted to do the same to him.

He pounded into her, hard and deep, the artistic finesse gone. Now only a rough drive to climax. She went over the edge before he did, her body clasping around him. Nothing else was real, just Renard, Renard Mauricette, his muscles, his hair, the flashing eyes, the sun-browned skin. He seemed more savage than man, and Eva had sworn to love both to the end of time.

In the throes of climax she felt limitless. They were crushed together, speared on the other, locked in an embrace that blurred the two like paint on a canvas. She could only gasp his name and hold onto him like an anchor in the storm they both created. And then, the ending. For it always had to end. He burst inside her with a hot groan, his breath quickening.

He sank into the bed still on top of her.

"Eva," he said, after a moment.

"Yes, Renard."

"You know I damn well love you."

"I love you."

"And you know what else?"

"What?"

"You were right. To not have to hide you- that's the greatest gift. To have you on my arm. The creoles can say what they like about us. I don't care. I don't care about anything when I am with you, but making you happy."

Rarely did Renard expose his feelings like this. And rarer still did the look in his eyes, devoid of any ironic amusement, speak with such intensity. She drew back, half-startled.

"I will have you," he said, "any way I can. Let's stay here."

A parrot screeched outside the window. They could hear the exhausted surf sucking at the beach, a ways off. Locals called this area of the island *Balenbouche*, 'whale's mouth', in the creole language. Perhaps Eva had been Jonah, being delivered to a foreign shore by forces beyond her ken.

And like Jonah, she had work here to do. There was doctoring to be done among the people of the island, who had even less than they out in her own home country. She might have a chance at happiness with Renard here. The lines of class and color blurred more freely on the French islands- it had always been that way. In public she might still look out of place on Renard's arm- but such an oddity could be navigated.

And it reminded her of Louisiana. The flowers. The breeze. The mangrove-stink on the air, the trill of birdsong. Life here never divided itself; time stretched out, all days feeling like they had blended into a single, long afternoon. The islanders moved slowly in all things. They valued rest.

Eva liked it very much.

There was still the question of money.

"Your associates," she said carefully, "In Boston..."

Renard pulled Eva on top of him and patted her rump. "Two things I am very good at, Eva, Cherie. Much like my French ancestors."

"What?"

"Making love," he said, "And making money. I don't know if you know this. I don't know if you are aware—but you've gone and married a very smart man. And also a very rich man."

"Oh?"

"Sure," grinned Renard. "Say the word, Eva, and we

can put roots down here as long as you like. I've already thought of several ideas since being here on how I can get started. You can do your little doctoring. I can do my ventures. And if you get tired, and you miss freezing your ass off in Boston, I can accommodate that too."

She snorted. "You really like it here?"

"More than I can say," he admitted. "And to be honest, my leg has never felt better."

Sam was not long on the island before he took up with the city boys, who at first tried to bully him, then learned their lesson and became his friend. He had some carpentry skills which made him usefully employed and gave him excuses to be down in the port town as often as he could. From the inner city he gravitated to the port itself, and soon he was spending every moment of his time at the shipyard.

The sailors, with their rough ways, developed sense of tragedy and elastic humor appealed to him. They reminded him of the men of Rue Cher. Not hung up on life at all. Still filled with mystery and wonder.

And it wasn't long before he approached Renard and asked for a small loan so he might join a crew and be a sailor.

Renard of course obliged, but Eva was displeased.

"Oh Sam," she kept saying. "You wanted to be a doctor. What happened?"

"I still do," he insisted. "Just- not now. Not right now. Look at you, Eva. You didn't do nothin' until you got older. I got time. I'm tired of stayin' in one place for good. I feel if I stay here I'm likely to fade away."

"We could send you back," she offered, feeling guilty. But Sam shook his head vehemently.

369

"Oh, no. I got no inclination to go back. Here I ain't got much, but I feel somethin' like a man. Ain't nothin' for me in America but the same old system. I'm tired of beggin' for a place at the table. I feel to make my own way."

So a sailor Sam would be. The loan secured, he left on a cargo ship set for England that sailed out on his sixteenth birthday. The last sight they caught of him he was waving a hat that was white as his teeth. He looked tall and strong against the Caribbean sky. His dark skin shone with happiness. The ship peeled out of the harbor like a slow leviathan, and Sam's waving grew weaker, and soon he disappeared from sight.

Eva was inconsolable.

"I failed him," she said to Renard miserably.

"He's going sailing, not to prison," said Renard. "Lots of young men go sailing."

"You could have trained him-" she said, reproachful. "Taken him under your wing more..."

"Sam is young," said Renard firmly. "But he knows what he wants. He doesn't want to be beholden to me. He wants to carve his path. It's his right, as a man. You know that, Eva."

Eva shook her head, and Renard led her away from the port.

"Auntie!" cried little Henri. "When Sam coming back?"

The impressionable child's mind had already began to pick up the colloquial speech of the islanders.

"I dunno, sugar," said Eva. She blinked back tears and groped for the little boy's hand. "Hopefully soon."

She tilted her head up at the deep blue sky to stall her

tears, and the color reminded her for a startling moment of the blue shade of Nelson's old hat. Her breath caught in her throat.

It was a lesson Eva would learn often over the years. That life, like the sea, would snatch things away. For a moment, for a season, for a decade. But it somehow, in little ways, in ships, in bottles, in memories as fleeting as a breeze or as strong as a trade wind, always brought them back.

She received the letter from Sam eight months later. By then she and Renard were expecting their first child.

They read it together on the balcony of the house Renard had built, with its view of the Caribbean Sea. Hard to believe the coast of Louisiana touched that same sea. That only a boat ride away were the horrors of the South, the land Eva had sold and would never again return to, and the memories of another time.

"He seems happy," said Eva, referencing the letter.

"I told you," said Renard. He wrapped his hands around her waist- a difficult thing. The baby would be a big one. He kissed her neck.

"Are you happy?" Eva asked him.

Renard said, "Yes. Of course."

Made in the USA
Middletown, DE
23 November 2020